GU00806422

Bianca Rosa Hart

Treasures of Darkness

Forgiveness and reconciliation are life
and their denial is death

YPS
York Publishing Services

First published 2017
Filippo del Re Publishing
© Cecilia Clementel Jones

Typesetting and Graphic design Andrea Nicolai | Francesca Bossini
Printing and distribution by York Publishing Services, York UK.

Cecilia Clementel Jones has asserted her right under the Copyright Design and Patents act, 1988, to be identified as the author of this work.

Every reasonable effort has been made to trace copyright holders of material reproduced in this book, but if any have been inadvertently overlooked the Publisher would like to hear from them.

All rights reserved. No part of this publication may be reproduced or transmitted in any form or by any means, electronic or mechanical, including photocopying, recording, or any information, storage or retrieval system without prior permission in writing from the publisher.

No responsibility for loss caused to any individual or organisation acting on or refraining from action as a result of the material in this publication can be accepted by YPS or this book's copyright holder.

British Library Cataloguing-in-Publication Data
A catalogue record for this book is available from the British Library
ISBN   978 1 9999227 0 2

TABLE OF CONTENTS

INTRODUCTION

I found this manuscript abandoned on a train seat when travelling on an East coast train in England. I looked for the Author's address so that I might return it to her but found only a pen name. It seemed to be a script for the theatre or television containing essays connected to several issues more or less related to the subject of the script.

The Author must have spent a long time correcting it. I felt sorry for her, wondering if this was her best copy and concluded that if I had it inexpensively published, which one can do nowadays, she may come upon it and recognize it. This story is loosely based on a cycle of historical novels by Winston Graham narrating the life of an impoverished Cornish squire Captain Ross Poldark. This script changes the ending of the seventh novel *The Angry Tide* by W. Graham published in 1977 into a completely different narrative. The first seven novels were published by the mid-fifties and were the subject of a popular television production in 1975-1977. The last three novels start with the birth of a child, Valentine, to Elizabeth and George Warleggan and close with the death of Elizabeth after her third childbirth.

Treasures of darkness

This is my third book and very different from the previous two: *this is my book*. I feel the urge to write now after my birthday party more than ever before. I often experience strands of thoughts ambling through my mind stumbling over one another; they join and dance together coming in fast like a shoal of fish and like fish they can swim away and slip through one's hands.

This writing aims to reinstate in 21st century words the interaction of truth and evil in an European culture with invisible extensive roots in western Christianity.

The start was chaotic: the images in my mind taking on a life of their own and writing their story were unbending to reason and for the first three months almost hallucinatory. I have always lived inside my head more than anywhere else (bad for driving a car on the M25 I can tell you) but what was happening this August bore urgency.

It reminded me of the image on the front cover of a childhood book I still own: *La capanna dello zio Tom (Uncle Tom's Cabin)*. It shows a woman with a baby in her arms jumping from one ice sheet to another, crossing a river as the ice is breaking: the desperate attempt of a fugitive slave in nineteenth century Virginia to escape her hunters (no one in their right mind would risk their life to follow her). She leaps until she reaches the safety of the other bank where the Friends (the Quaker railroad organisation helping fugitives) are waiting for her.

Elizabeth must not die

Watching the Poldark serial on BBC1 this winter (2015) I was captured by the intensity of the love story of a fearless rebellious hero and a Cinderella born to be a Lady (Demelza his wife). I downloaded the first seven novels on my tablet, then some Poldark novels written later; the last one when Graham was 90! I read them in my usual fashion: bitty, fast, going over and over the pages, with the feeling I was missing the paper, the smell, the book binding. I was moved by the tension between George and Ross. Tales of young bucks locking horns over the same fragile doe mostly irritate me, being neither fragile nor by any stretch of the imagination a doe; this one however thrust a hook into my fantasy. Graham's writing is crafted so that one is given clear but sparse, scattered cues to the character's personality and machinations, like finding bits of a mosaic scattered around the garden. The hero may be a self-portrait of the Author and I have an idea that George Warleggan was a real person too closely observed by and closely connected to Winston Graham.

Ross and Demelza are in full view in the foreground together with Elizabeth and Cousin Francis Poldark, George slowly materialising from the shadows a polite bon vivant morphing into a pitiless, dour shark who is also coveting the doe: Elizabeth. The violent Atlantic tide (*The Angry Tide* is the title of the seventh novel bringing the cycle to a close) is a metaphor for the unravelling of the parallel story of two couples who both reconcile, one to be struck by death and decay the other (Ross and Demelza) blossoming into happiness and life. The reconciliation between George and Elisabeth is clearly present in their last dialogue. Satisfyingly both men eat humble pie[1].

George is punished by Elisabeth's death, not that he is able to grasp it since emotional intelligence is a neglected area of this formidable character. After her death he states to Ross as if unaware of what he is saying "look what WE have brought her to!" I started to feel a little sorry for George in view of the fact (Elizabeth knows) he has actually been cheated with a son, Valentine, who was fathered by his sworn enemy, Ross, during – this is skated over in the original

---

1   Umbles are the venison's offal, made into a pie to be eaten by servants after the hunt. The phonetics help the phrase "eat h/umble pie" slide into a figurative meaning: take an inferior or humble position, such as admitting to a mistake.

novel in true masculine style – a rape, however gentlemanly it may have ended. The story starts with a young soldier Captain Ross Poldark, an impoverished Cornish squire, returning home after having fought and lost against British colonists intent on becoming citizens of the United States. His cheek is marked by a scar and one of his legs is lame. His father has died and the girl he had hoped to marry, the beautiful aristocratic Elizabeth, is about to marry Francis Poldark his cousin. His involvement with mining on his land and a joint business venture see him on a collision course with his contemporary the elegant and rich George Warleggan, only son and heir of Nicholas Warleggan who owns a bank, mines and a smelting business[2]. George persuades Cousin Francis to give him the (confidential) list of Ross' business associates and is able to put such financial pressure on them that they desist from the venture. When a Warleggan owned ship is wrecked on Nampara's beach (owned by Ross) and looted by the villagers – as was the custom – Ross is charged with inciting a riot and tried (courtesy of George) but acquitted. In the meantime he has on impulse married a servant in his house, Demelza, a miner's daughter, a spirited bright woman very much in love with him. He will find happiness with her but their first girl will soon die of an infectious illness.

The feud with George continues and their conflict is such that on more than one occasion physical violence erupts, Ross being the first to lose his temper. George is emotionally controlled and devious ("He watched him like a snake"). He has a chip on his shoulder about being the grandson of a poor blacksmith; Ross, a landowning squire, has an ancient name. Francis overcome with guilt for the betrayal of his Cousin breaks his ties with George and becomes involved with Ross in a mining venture that later looks like a failure. He is also impoverished having gambled away money and will later drown in their mine leaving Elizabeth a widow with one son and ailing parents. Ross has never entirely forgotten his first love and George is now skilfully wooing her. Demelza fears for her marriage as she has always felt inferior to Elizabeth. The coveted prey, overcome by the financial strain and loneliness, agrees to marry George. Ross, beside himself at such news, appears one evening at the door of her bedroom and starts asking question about the engagement but ends up raping her. On reflection he decides that he wishes to stay married to Demelza; at this point the failing mine begins to be very lucrative. He cannot face meeting Elizabeth again and she will soon marry a triumphant George but she is pregnant – Ross being the father. She falls down the stairs and the child is born (so everyone believes) premature. Many other characters and couples, from all walks of life, come into view in this vast historical tableau. I shall only mention the mine's doctor who is Ross' friend,

---

2   Copper and tin mining started in Cornwall in prehistoric times.

Dwight Enys, who marries a local heiress Caroline.

After four years George's suspicion about Valentine's paternity is roused by the dying words of the Poldark maiden aunt (aunt Agatha) who lives with them and has always been a thorn in his side. George and Ross (after his financial situation has improved) metaphorically cross swords due to George's political ambitions: in a local election to Parliament Ross wins and becomes MP for Truro (that means the MP for Lord Falmouth, a position previously occupied by his rival). George then buys himself a different parliamentary seat using political power to further his interests. At the beginning of *The Angry Tide* both couples are in London; one of George's cronies called Monk Adderley (another MP) tries to seduce Demelza then challenges Ross to a duel (an illegal act at the time). The duel remains secret but Ross is badly wounded and his opponent dies; Demelza rushes back to Cornwall. We hear that Elizabeth is pregnant again but her marriage is collapsing: George cannot contain his morbid jealousy and his doubts about Valentine's paternity.

A Lutheran Pastor and a German Prince

And now, as Monty Python would have it, for something completely different and unexpected: a Lutheran Pastor and theologian killed on Hitler's orders (together with admiral Canaris and other members of their secret resistance cell); one of many cruelly meaningless executions a few days before the end of the third Reich. One of his books was a gift for my birthday. Here too I was bowled over (books can do this to me) and within a month I had bought Bonhoeffer's basic five or six books. I read two recent biographies of Pastor Dietrich Bonhoeffer (1906-1945) a brilliant theologian and a talented piano player, golden child of the German intellectual elite taken in the vortex of history: the fast flowing tragedy of the German people and the crushing of opposition to Hitler in the University and the Churches. I now had an imaginary companion to discuss evil and the third Rich with. He was, I felt, a German "Prince" a brilliant mind, highly sensitive and steeped in Hochkultur[3].

This led me back to a former interest in the Nuremberg trials: the psychological elaboration and ethical reflection of the very few protagonists of the Third Reich who were prepared to accept some responsibility for that calamity, one of whom was Albert Speer. Martin Heidegger one of the greatest philosophers of his age,

---

3   High culture. The humanistic, philosophical literary and artistic culture requiring intensive training and some maintenance of the bourgeois, military and aristocratic establishment in Europe, the German version in this case, consolidated around the end of the nineteenth century and transmitted through elitist education.

author of *Being and Time*, having colluded with Hitler's regime with intellectual enthusiasm maintained, after the Second World War, a pointed and probably unrepentant silence.

The connection between my social history readings and all the imaginary humans from the Poldark novels crisscrossing at will my inner world is the theme of evil; how to retrace one's steps, "Having lost their heads and lost their Bible" (Bonhoeffer's pithy sentence on the best and brightest in the Lutheran church colluding with the Nazi's ideological and physical assault). It is worth noting that colluding Lutherans and intellectuals during the initial phases of Nazi-Fascism, when it was conquering the hearts and minds of an impoverished and humiliated, proud German nation, were swiftly discarded (sometimes even imprisoned) when the regime unveiled its criminal, predatory nature.

The human and Christian question of truth and the courage to defend it or how to return to justice in repentance is what we need to work out for this new century. Bonhoeffer for me is more than just one of the most influential theologians of the 20th century; he also stands on the threshold of the 21st century with a firm, cutting thrust[4]. The other core reference here is the French philosopher and psychoanalyst Paul Ricoeur who debates the theme of evil from a Christian perspective.

Responsibility, Retribution, Reconciliation

Albert Speer, Hitler's architect, explains how admissions of guilt mean nothing and are at best only a beginning. Fest, the book's author, who had helped Speer to edit his memoirs, had conversations about him with Hugh Trevor-Roper (Oxford academic and historian of the Third Reich) who believes that Speer did not even make it to base camp of admission of personal guilt. "He (Trevor-Roper) suddenly felt a void open up behind all the intellectual sharpness and clarity. Speer was certainly not corrupt, nor malicious, hard-hearted, base or whatever. He was something far worse: hollow" p.179[5]. Here the historian is commenting on the BBC broadcast during which he had discussed the Nazi regime 25 years after its fall, in the company of Albert Speer and John Kenneth Galbraith amongst others. I think the story goes that Galbraith had discussed (before the Nuremberg trials of 1945) at length with Speer (in custody) how he had man-

---

4   The Valdese Theologian Paolo Ricca (in the hundred[th] anniversary the theologian's birth) writes in 2006: "He was not born one hundred years *before* us, he was born one hundred years *after* us, we are only trying to run after him" – my translation from Italian: "Non è nato cento anni *prima* di noi, è nato cento anni *dopo* di noi, e noi lo stiamo rincorrendo".

5   Fest, J. 2007.

aged the considerable feat of maintaining the German industry working well nearly to the end despite allied bombing and difficulties with supplies of materials. Workers on the other hand would have been no problem as they came from concentration camps or were press ganged Europeans, all treated very badly. The person who furnished him with workers was hanged at Nuremberg (Fritz Sauckel) and no one believed Speer when he said he did not know what the workers' conditions were (which he continued to maintain). My suspicion is he only got 20 years instead of a death sentence because he cooperated with Galbraith (and other inquisitive buddies) and because at the end he defied Hitler's scorched earth policies and (he said) planned to assassinate him. He cut a decent and dignified figure admitting that the (first) Nuremberg trial was necessary and his sentence justified "There is a common responsibility for such horrible crimes even in an authoritarian system" he reportedly stated, which is more than any of his co-defendants did[6]. It is, alas, common not personal responsibility (possibly he reflects on the latter in his *Spandau Diaries*; he served his 20 years sentence in Berlin's Spandau prison).

The problem is vaster than one man's uncomprehending obstinacy: Bonhoeffer who lived through the calamity being only twenty seven years old when Hitler came to power was quick to grasp the catastrophic implications and was aghast. Remember: Germany at the time was the flower of European civilisation with great minds, top scientists and the highest standards of education; then, in a matter of months, everything promptly fell apart with little or no resistance from the Churches, the Military, the Judiciary or the Universities. An entire civilised nation surrendered to a barbaric mass movement shielded by a criminal militia with the Great Man at the helm whilst other European States minded their own business.

According to Bonhoeffer the problem is as much stupidity as evil and he is sufficiently distraught to ask "Are we still of any use?"[7]. He is reflecting on the failure of the reasonable ones with the best intentions and naïve misreading of reality, leading them to be crushed by colliding forces without having accomplished anything at all[8]. For my generation, the Second World War was still alive in oral history; our parents did not talk about it much and at school history stopped abruptly with the firing of a pistol in Sarajevo in 1914 but everything around us spoke eloquently of the recent past.

---

6   Tusa A.T. 1984.

7   "We believed we would overcome on the basis of reason and justice. When both defaulted it seemed we had no resource left". Written in prison May 1944. Bonhoeffer D. 1988 p.368; initially published 1970 by Kaiser Verlag, Munchen.

8   Bonhoeffer, D. p.61ff. Ten years later written Christmas 1942 (Resistenza e Resa/Letters from Prison).

I think we should not forget this perennial problem of revenge, repentance, justice and forgiveness. It is multifaceted: legal and psychological, cultural and social, spiritual and religious. When we least expect it we may have to face the onslaught and the aftermath again and contemplate how (Bonhoeffer again) "A coming generation is to go on living".

Albert Speer stated that: "The real questions with which he had been wrestling begin only afterwards: how he became what he was, what life at home with his parents did to promote or discourage it, how one's reason can be blocked, how individuals or ideas can gain power over people and what should be done to counter it. Or how one can go through life unmolested as a split personality without even noticing the contradictions at the bottom of everything… Or how he has come to feel that the person he once was is a stranger whom he would just pass by in the street, without giving him a second glance… but no one was interested in such questions" he complained p.171[9]. To my psychotherapist's ear this suggests a combination of rationalisation and denial, despite one's agreement with the ideas put forward.

The plurality of the notion of justice must not be equated with moral relativism. A human society where, overtly or covertly, the powerful dominate and write the rules to suit themselves is walking down a tragic path. Justice cannot be based merely on rights and retribution or, worse, on retaliation. Freedom and justice are meaningful only in relation to others within a real community.

In the last generation, starting with the study of traditional reconciliation rituals in tribal societies, procedures described as **restorative justice**[10] have been applied within the legal system in Australian, African and South American countries. Highlighting the needs and power of the victim and based on the wrongdoer accepting responsibility restorative justice runs parallel to the Christian tradition of forgiveness without ignoring the need for repair and restitution. These practices have proven useful in juvenile justice and schools. The process of reconciliation in South Africa after the fall of the apartheid regime (the white population anticipating a bloodbath which did not materialise) was run on the lines of restorative justice and later imitated elsewhere. One of its leaders, Archbishop Desmond Tutu, affirmed that South Africa would have no future with a retaliatory justice, even if administered by the legal system where denying responsibility is a practical necessity (as was the case in Nuremberg). Only justice with reconciliation, repentance and repair could heal yesterday's evil. It is possible that this discourse may be used as veil for lack of a political will – or mandate – to punish those responsible who are denying their responsibility.

---

9   Fest J. 2007.

10   Broughton G. 2015.

In situations, not at all uncommon[11] where, as in Germany, Italy or France after the war, the number of people who have compromised themselves is very high and chaos threatens society's cohesion or even mere survival the lynching of some and the hanging of a few others does not seem an efficient justice. After the Second World War the vast majority of such wrongdoers staunchly maintained a denial of their responsibility in the face of damning evidence and continued to do so even after sentencing, even when freed from jail or by amnesty. When the risk of prosecution or punishment was not present they maintained their innocence, at times in the face of a strong personal rejection by their immediate family. Frankly a vast majority got away with it. This applies not only to Germany, (where a sustained and robust legal and cultural attempt to come to terms with the fascist past is evident from the seventies onwards) but also to several other European countries and to Japan.

Heritage within Modernity

The three strands in this human tale are: truth, individual and societal responsibility for sin (a word deserving to be resurrected), the Christian process of conversion compared to the humanistic ethos concerning psychological responses to personal and societal failings (here I am batting for both teams). Nietzsche pointed out: "If nothing is true, everything is permitted". Postmodernity fearlessly raises the stakes consigning consciousness and freedom of the will to the dustbins of history!

I am staking my Christian and western cultural heritage with modernity.

Look and see how often the human community dances with the devil and consider how to evade this embrace; did you ever notice, like Isaiah, God's justice falling like rains filling the earth? I suspect you did not but without it the human family is destroyed and the individual in despair is left alone with his failures.

The following biblical quote links God's infinite power and his justice.

Righteousness is raining down from heaven and filling the Earth. This shall not happen through holy or religious people (pious D. Bonhoeffer might call them) but through Cyrus, a king who does not even acknowledge the God of Israel. God through Cyrus, unknown to the king himself, fulfils His promise of Redemption and Salvation for his chosen people, Israel.

---

11   I have noted at least a dozen in my lifetime: Rwanda, South Africa, Vietnam, Cambodia, Iraq post Saddam, Greece, Argentina, Guatemala and Chile when the military dictatorships ended…

From the book of the prophet Isaiah chapter 45, vv. 2-5 & 6-9:

I will go before you
I will level the mountains
I will break down gates of bronze
And cut through gates of iron
I will give you the treasures of darkness[12]
Riches stored in secret places
So that you may know that I am the Lord…
Though you do not acknowledge me
I am the Lord, and there is no other
I form the light and create darkness[13]
I bring prosperity and create disaster
I, the Lord, do all these things.
You, heavens above, rain down righteousness
Let the clouds shower it down
Let the earth open wide
Let salvation spring up
Let righteousness grow with it
I, the Lord, have created it.

---

12   Hence the title of this book

13   Quoted at the end of *Act 2*. I interpret the statement as God taking responsibility for both good and evil present in this world.

Act 1

W. Graham resorts to a character's death on several occasions in the Poldark novels either when the conflict is hard to solve or merely when the character gets in the way of the story. Death does not bring closure; on the contrary it makes it impossible to unravel previous history and freezes memory making the resolution of conflict impossible. If Elizabeth dies all the characters closest to her story – Ross, George and Valentine – partly die with her. In the novel Ross is led by the shock of her death to a rambling reflection on loss and mortality: he imagines death dividing him and Demelza as he is unable to face his present loss of Elizabeth.
Here my different narrative begins (Act 1, b).

1a   Ext. A spring Day
George with his father, Nicholas[14]

George accompanies his father in his regular Sunday promenade; it leads to the cliffs after passing through meadows with flowers in bloom. He recalls sitting on the court bench together with father the previous week judging a farmer caught storing smuggled goods.

GEORGE
Father, on Thursday when we fined Sam Healey who had been found hiding smuggled bottles of brandy I imagined how dreadful it might be for one of us to find himself in the dock.

NICHOLAS
George, are you thinking of something you have done, while still within the limits of the law, which does not rest easy on your conscience?

GEORGE
I sometimes wonder whether I have a conscience at all.

---

14   This is a window into father's attempt to reassure George, troubled by fear of social censure. George's character shows some doubt, introspective effort leading to self-criticism. Here and later (2e) father is reluctant to engage deeply. George, it seems, can intimidate even his own father.

This reply warns Nicholas he is in uncharted waters and he replies cautiously:

NICHOLAS
You are a respectable, upright and law-abiding person. You appear to be.

GEORGE *replies, in a strained voice*
I may indeed appear to be pliable, pleasant and charming when I need to in order to reach my aim which I always do.

NICHOLAS *in agreement*:
We all further our projects as best we can and enjoy success.

GEORGE, *angrily*
I know, but such is my need to win that no holds are barred: I can cheat or apply pressure even financial blackmail; it shall not trouble my sleep or my digestion.

NICHOLAS, *with authority, soothingly*
My son when I have seen you stray beyond the bounds I felt a gentleman should not breach I have always pointed it out. Now that you are an adult I trust you to be able to judge where fairness lays. I wish your path be honourable as well as strictly legal.

GEORGE, *exasperated, fearing his message is not heard*
I feel at times that the needle of my moral compass is not due north but bobs in every direction to serve my desires. I cannot trust anyone: I need to tie up, control and yoke even my friends.

NICHOLAS *reassuring, but missing the point*
True friends you need not tie, they follow you freely. They have chosen and like you for the elegant, witty and successful gentleman you are.

GEORGE
That's how I appear yet were I another I would not choose George as my friend. I can see hidden dark caves in my soul.

NICHOLAS *They are now in view of the sea standing on the edge of the cliff*
No other will see or enter such caves unless you allow them. Look in if you will, but be careful. If you gaze into the abyss the abyss may gaze into you[15].

---

15 A quote from F. Nietzsche.

GEORGE

> Father, I am trying to block the entrance to the caves. There are many points of entry into the darkness, above water and below, I may even fall in from the cliff face

NICHOLAS

> Do not walk these cliffs alone you may need help. Should you fall you know you can always count on me.

The conversation stops abruptly both fearing to step further. They pause at the cliff's edge before turning back watching the seagulls floating on the waves.

Camera lingers on seascape – the sounds of nature in the background.

Elizabeth's words

In Graham's original novel, *The Angry Tide*, let us pay attention to the two final dialogues between Elizabeth and George, before and after the child's birth. The latter dialogue is the one in which George finally accepts that Valentine is his child because the new born girl is also premature as a consequence of the potion Elizabeth bought in London and took to hasten the birth. *The Angry Tide* closes with Elizabeth's death from gangrene due to the ergot in the potion; at the dawn of the nineteenth century marking the end of the first cycle of the Poldark novels. In their last dialogue (the notes in brackets are mine), after the childbirth (deceptively delivery appears to have gone well), George finally accepts that Valentine is his child and says "Now at last I can see I was wrong *[Elizabeth knows he is right]* clearly it has done damage to our marriage. I trust it is not beyond repair *[Elizabeth thinks: so is the hard man tamed]*. Now that I can put this out of my mind – however much I might regret it was ever allowed to enter – it happened. I cannot – no one ever can – withdraw the past. Elizabeth. I have to say I have been at fault in all this. Perhaps now – from now on… some of the unhappiness can be forgiven… the disagreeable times forgot. She squeezed his hand "Go and look at our daughter". In the previous dialogue, before Elizabeth takes the potion, George fighting with his anger says through gritted teeth: "You must know it Elizabeth! You are the only person I have cared about". This spark of love, wrapped in possessive jealousy, is the narrow passage we can take to rescue George's humanity and his soul.

Not far from them a parallel but very different reconciliation scene is taking place between Ross and Demelza. The he-goat devil described by Ross at the close of

The Four Swans[16], a vengeful God, does not take such last-minute adjustments into account and strikes the innocent (well, nearly innocent) victim with death thereby punishing the two men. George's pithy statement to Ross after Elizabeth's death is astonishingly accurate **"Go on you scum George shouted. Go up and see her! See what WE have brought her to!"**.

A bright, observant man, I think George knows and has always known ever since Aunt Agatha crafted with her dying words her terrible revenge[17], perhaps even before, that Valentine may not be his child. Now, looking at baby Ursula, their child, he is prepared to enter the game of deception that must be played lest their marriage collapses.

The only other way out is truth; a tragic truth must force itself on several people bent on avoiding it. Elizabeth, in a delirious state, will speak the truth to both men who need respond to it personally and within their relationship.

1b   Int. Trentwith's parlour Early evening
Elizabeth, Dwight, George, Ross, Servants

The study (or parlour) is close to the bedroom; the action taking place in the latter is often off scene[18].
Dwight, having attended the birth, emerges from Elizabeth's bedroom and enters into the parlour informing George that he is the father of a little girl.

DWIGHT

My sincere congratulations. This is your wife's third confinement and the baby, being only seven months, was an easy delivery. Madam should rest one week at least; a wet nurse will be needed for the baby, she seems healthy but will be delicate. At present I must deliver the afterbirth and foresee no difficulties. Allow me to return and see to this.

George nods in reply
Elizabeth in bed, the baby in a cot by the window: Elizabeth is shaking and sweating, the pain and the fear have left her and she notices she is alone with the doctor:

---

16   Graham W. 1977, *The Four Swans*.

17   The Poldark maiden great aunt Agatha on her deathbed suggested to George that Valentine may have been a full-term baby, therefore conceived before the marriage.

18   Camera position: the bedroom door should be visible from the study/parlour and some scenes are filmed from there with shots including the bedroom door. The door frame is symbolic of a border between reality and hallucination, birth and death, silence and avowal.

ELIZABETH

Dwight I have something to say in private.

(He pushes the door to and she hands him a green bottle)

This remedy was given to me by a doctor in London. I requested a potion that would cause a premature delivery. I took four spoonfuls last night and it worked. I was told to inform the doctor attending the delivery but you must keep it a secret.

DWIGHT *looks at the label and is shocked*

Did he tell how dangerous this potion could be?

ELIZABETH

Yes, I was warned but I had no option. In the same way as the baby was trapped in my womb so have I been trapped for several years now, this drug was the only dangerous road to freedom. What is the risk?

DWIGHT

You and the baby may die! I shall not leave until I am satisfied that you are safe… Why would you wish for a premature delivery?

Having revealed one secret Elizabeth feels inclined to confide more, the relaxing effect of the laudanum[19] taking over her mind and body. She had felt so utterly alone in her fight to defend Valentine.

ELIZABETH

George doubts that Valentine was one month premature, had he been born full term he could not have been George's child.

DWIGHT

And is he?

ELIZABETH

Dwight this question cannot be asked nor answered. When George sees this child is premature he will be reassured that Valentine was too. I am concerned that George has been ignoring Valentine or, following his moods, warming to the child when his suspicion subsides. Valentine's mind is turning from anger to joy to confusion. He asked me if papa thinks he is very naughty; I see his unhappiness and fear George's brooding moods like storm clouds ready to burst in fits of jealousy. I have tried to free him of suspicion as he also suffers, loving me and his child.

---

19   Laudanum contained opioids

DWIGHT
Could you not free him madam with the truth?

ELIZABETH *sadly*
Truth is a hail of arrows on us both, and on another as well.

ELIZABETH *becomes distressed as Dwight eases out the remains of the placenta, the baby whimpers.*
May she be happy…and safe.

GEORGE O/S *knocks at the door*
All being well I'd like to thank my wife and spend some time in private with her. Dr. Behenna has now arrived; you may wish to talk with him[20].

Dwight takes these words as a request to leave, he now needs to consult his colleague on potential complication due to the ergot in the potion and he quickly realises that Behenna is also aware of the doubts surrounding Valentine's birth. (The doctors are seen talking but their words are not heard).

When George emerges from his wife's room he looks content when walking to meet the two doctors waiting in the parlour:
GEORGE
I presume Doctor Behenna can now take over, is there any reason for concern?
He adds, noting the worried look on Dwight's face.

DWIGHT
I noticed your wife continues to shiver. A hot bath may help her.
Dwight enters the bedroom and then emerges saying with a firm voice:
Madam took a cordial and I am concerned possible harm may come from it; I would, with your consent, stay awhile longer. Please ask the servant to fetch hot water.

More than the words the tone of the doctor's voice alarms George.
GEORGE
Which cordial do you mean and by whom procured, do you know anything

---

20 The dialogue described in Graham's book as taking place between Elizabeth and George after the baby's birth during which Elizabeth gives Ursula her name takes place at this point, see p.18 here.

about this Behenna? Where is the bottle now? On whose advice… or did she…?

DWIGHT, *searching for words*

We are not clear how much danger there is but we shall try to deal with it together, I must add that some information I obtained from your wife regarding the cordial is confidential. Let us make sure she is kept warm and comfortable, within one day the danger will be over.

GEORGE

This happy birth…Now you tell me my wife may be in danger but cannot say why, I require answers! What cordial did she take? Was it in her cabinet?

This is the unfortunate moment chosen by Ross to slide past the entrance and enlist a servant to show him in the parlour. Mechanically the men bow slightly and Ross politely apologises for intruding.
Ross

My sincere apologies if my arrival is inconvenient. I was concerned that the presence of two doctors may indicate a difficult birth. Was the mother safely delivered?

DWIGHT *replies in a similarly formal manner:*

Yes, she has given birth to a healthy girl and I am about to depart leaving her in the care of Behenna. Shall we withdraw together?

His haste to slip away is so evident that George becomes suspicious and speaks to Ross in an almost welcoming tone.
GEORGE

Let us finish the conversation you interrupted, Ross. I was having a difference of opinion with Enys, your friend which you may help us with. *Without waiting for an answer he added.* The good doctor tells me Elizabeth has taken a cordial which may cause complications but he cannot give me details as he would be disclosing a patient's confidential information. What do you say?

Ross

Not being a doctor myself I might solicit the opinion of two medical men. What matters is the good health of the mother.

Behenna prudently disappears inside Elizabeth's bedroom[21]; a servant is seen leaving the

---

21   The camera, filming from the parlour, should focus on the image of the bedroom door frame, thus linking the voice of Elizabeth, unseen, to Ross in the parlour and George moving between the

bedroom Behenna hurriedly returns to the parlour.

BEHENNA *to Dwight*

I think she has taken a turn for the worse: her legs are cold and clammy to the touch.

DWIGHT *to George*

I fear we must face the complication I mentioned.

GEORGE

I believe we must search the cabinet for this cordial. *George moves directly into the room followed by the two doctors whilst Ross stays in the parlour looking perplexed. The conversation from the bedroom can be heard by Ross who is pacing irritably.*

GEORGE O/S

Easily found. Now the label here says er... ergot... never heard of it. Can you please explain?

BEHENNA O/S

That's it, she took ergot. The drug, an extract from rye, causes contractions of the womb. Rather risky!

DWIGHT O/S

And contractions of the blood vessels which may be a danger to her life[22]. At least we delivered the child.

GEORGE O/S

Why should Elizabeth wish for a premature delivery?

BEHENNA O/S

This question I believe you can answer better than I could[23].

---

bedroom and the parlour.

22   Ergot has been used for many centuries but I am not sure how much doctors knew about its effects at the time. An opinion from someone specialising in History of Medicine would be useful. I later have Dwight using amyl nitrate, a vasodilator discovered in the middle of the nineteenth century in Paris. One either makes it up, as I am doing, on the basis of scant remains of my medical training, or seeks an expert opinion. One needs a contemporary remedy that could have counteracted the contractions in the blood vessels leading to gangrene.

23   Behenna can speak more freely now that the servants have left to prepare the bath water.

GEORGE O/S
> What do you mean?

BEHENNA O/S
> I recall a conversation you and I had not long ago and I trust Enys is as mindful of keeping confidential information as I am myself[24].

Ross' face shows increasing tension. Noting how he has been forgotten he goes to pick up his hat with the intention of departing but comes to a halt hearing Elizabeth scream.

ELIZABETH O/S
> No, Ross, no… you cannot possibly! You must stop. How dare you in my own bedroom. For shame… I'll scream.
> *Her voice increases ending in a shrill:*
> You would not dare... Ross Poldark!

The blood rises to Ross' face for a moment then he loses colour and becomes pale. Behenna standing next to Elisabeth is pushed violently away by her and can be seen clutching the door frame. Ross slowly moves towards a chair and hears Dwight's voice.

DWIGHT O/S
> She is delirious[25].
> *Dwight then slides out of the door angrily gesturing to Ross that he should go but Ross has frozen. When Dwight physically tries to push Ross out of the parlour and lead him downstairs George notices it and moves towards them swiftly addressing Ross in a controlled sarcastic tone:*

GEORGE
> Ah, Ross Poldark, well met. Need a glass of brandy?
> *Having poured liquor into a glass George throws its content in Ross' face. Ross who is standing with his hat in his hands collapses onto the chair and takes out his handkerchief trying to wipe his face.*

DWIGHT
> Now, now Mr Warleggan your wife is delirious and her life may be in danger, lesser matters can wait *Turning again to Ross he says with a commanding tone* Ross, go, NOW.

---

24 George had some months earlier questioned Behenna in private about Valentine's prematurity, threatening him to keep such a conversation a secret.

25 Delirium was a possible effect of ergot poisoning.

ROSS, *unsteady*
  Whatever else I may be, I am no coward.
He continues to wipe his face mechanically.

GEORGE, *starting in a low voice but ending in dull rage*
  What else may you be? The ravisher of a defenceless woman who was promised
  to me!

*Ross sinks further into the chair, his head bowed but trying to regain his composure with
slow movements of his hands. He is ashen faced and Dwight stands with his back to him
as if trying to protect him, facing George.*
DWIGHT *in a cold professional tone to George:*
  We must increase Elizabeth's blood flow which is now reduced by a constriction
  of the vessels. I have recently tried a new drug which relieves angina called amyl
  nitrate, it works by dilating the arteries. If you agree we can try a small dose. I
  am confident it will do no harm and it may improve her condition, let's attend
  to your wife if Behenna agrees with my suggestion.

GEORGE *moves back into the bedroom*
  Behenna what is your reply?

BEHENNA O/S *in a firm, cold voice:*
  We really must keep her warm and, yes, I know the drug. I used it myself to treat
  a patient with angina recently with good results. I believe I have some in my case;
  it must be placed under the tongue.

GEORGE
  Very well then.

GEORGE *is standing in the doorway, his hands folded behind his back, visible from the
parlour. Without turning he adds slowly.*
  And I think doctor Enys is also right in saying that Ross should go home now.
*Getting up Ross makes a slight bow in his direction and turns to leave, as he walks out
George turns slowly and in his low growl adds with force:*
  And reflect on the consequences of his sin!

1c   Int. Nampara's library Night-time
Ross & Dwight

In the early hours of the next day Dwight walked into the library where Ross was resting on the sofa, a pair of candles illuminating his desk.

DWIGHT

Elizabeth's condition has taken a turn for the worse, I shall return to Trentwith tomorrow, I need the rest. We may lose her, George has been by her side all along. I suggest you pray for her life.

ROSS *looking very tired*

What good would it do? If she dies George shall kill me, if she lives he'll hate me more than ever knowing I took her by force and Valentine is possibly my son.

DWIGHT

You could pray for yourself. Pray that God help you reason with George who will surely need an explanation. Perhaps I do too: could you tell me what really caused her distress? Her delirious words painted a scene; is it memory, imagination, desire?

ROSS, *with an anguished voice*

She repeated almost word for word what she said on that night, it stunned me. We met one month before she was married, there was no witness. I was so angry with both of them I ravished her. Afterwards I stayed and we managed to talk in a civilized fashion but I never went back I did not contact her nor did I ever ask for forgiveness. It was the lawless Ross that pushed his way into her bedroom. That was not really me but some twin shadow... I never thought, I know it is absurd, but I never thought she might become pregnant. I have heard women are more likely to be with child if they are...raped.
Ross sobs briefly.

DWIGHT *picks a large Bible and leafs through it*

This is something I have read and repeated to myself. It helped my grief and shame after Karen was killed. King David speaks to God as if the Lord were a powerful and loving friend whom he has angered[26]:

> Have mercy on me, O God, according to thy loving kindness;
> according unto the multitude of thy tender mercies blot out my transgressions
> Wash me thoroughly from mine iniquity and cleanse me from my sin
> For I acknowledge my transgressions and my sin is ever before me
> Against thee, thee only have I sinned and done this evil in thy sight

---

26   Psalm 51 Miserere: when the prophet Nathan came to him after David had committed adultery with Bathsheba (King's James Bible).

That thou mightiest be justified when thou speakest, and be clear when Thou
judgest.
Try it Ross: "Have mercy on me O God, according to thy loving kindness…"

*A naïve suggestion? Ross would try anything that may relieve him from this crushing
blow, from his fear.*

Ross
Have mercy on me Lord according to thy loving kindness…
(after a long pause)
For I acknowledge my transgressions and my sin is ever before me.

Dwight *putting a hand on his shoulder*
According unto the multitude of thy tender mercies blot out my transgressions…

Ross *retorts irritably*
Do you really think George or Elizabeth will forgive me? God may be in heaven
and we are down here. She is dying; there is nothing I can do.

Dwight
We can ask God for a sign of his forgiveness: that Elizabeth may live. She thought
if she had a premature birth this time George would be convinced Valentine was
also premature, that he was his child. She is risking her life for Valentine.

Ross
For nothing, now George knows.

Dwight
I should not tell you this, Ross, and I trust you will tell no one else. George was
at her bedside asking her forgiveness for hounding her with his suspicion, for his
refusal to speak to Valentine and for being an unpleasant bully to both. He said
something like "I was poisoned by jealousy and I became poisonous". Now I
know you are innocent my angel, you were taken by force. The child is innocent
too. My behaviour towards you both has been intolerable. If you live and forgive
me I shall change for you". He continued in this vein for a while. It is fortunate
Behenna dismissed the servants just in time to stop them hearing all that took
place. George turned to me and said: "Ross is a reckless cad but he was provoked,
I hounded him mercilessly. A masterstroke this: my honour, my wife's honour,
the Warleggan's heir all stained; my marriage wounded, my wife dying to protect her child, Valentine, distressed by what his papa is doing to him hating and
loving him in the same breath…"; suddenly he became angry with you saying:

"By the time I am finished with him Ross will wish he were dead!"

Ross, *in a resigned tone*

I suppose I'd feel the same if I were in his place. Still, this is a lot better than I anticipated. We may be able to reason.

DWIGHT

I believe, my friend, a very angry George will confront you and you must be prepared for it. It might be better to meet with no witness present if you both give your word you will not kill each other!

Ross

What shall I tell Demelza?

DWIGHT

What does she know so far?

Ross

Everything, except for the fact that Elizabeth did not consent. I was (and still am) too ashamed to tell her.

DWIGHT

If you allow me I shall tell her what happened at Trentwith this evening, giving her this information as if she knew it already. I know how close you two are, I see you keep no secrets from each other.

Ross

Please do so. I am worried George may also target my family. I can't face anybody at present, nor him nor Demelza. If it is a cold clear morning I may go to watch the sea. Wish to run away. NO! Turn and face it, face George, face Elizabeth may she live! Let me know.

DWIGHT *embraces him and leaves*

I shall. I must go now. May God forgive you and give you peace.

1d   Ext. Nampara's beach The hour before dawn
George, Ross

For this section the music is a crucial leitmotiv. Verbal and non-verbal communication is set against a background of nature: a cold and crisp December dawn with a calm sea. The Atlantic tide will take them by surprise despite their looking out for it. A barely noticeable crescendo in the music, like the invisible swelling tide. I suggest Sibelius' Karelia.

Seagull's cries are to be used as a fear level indicator: louder escalating cries when the anger or fear grow. The dawn chorus signifies lowered tension. It is first light, a few clouds veiling the moon, very cold and dry but not windy, birds are starting their dawn chorus.

Ross *is sitting on one side of the boat and looking out to sea. He bows his head slightly and says slowly audibly*

Have mercy on me, God, according to thy loving kindness and cleanse me from my sin.

George, who has walked towards the boat silently slows down and reveals surprise. He waits a short while then coughs to signal his presence and walks towards the boat saying:
GEORGE, *confidently*

Good day. Mind if I sit on your beach with you? When you've finished your present conversation we need to talk.

Ross, *tense*

Well, God does not seem to be at home.

GEORGE, *teasing*

Maybe he was not expecting you to call. I presume neither of us had much sleep the night just past.

Ross

How is Elizabeth?

GEORGE

Out of danger. She is asleep. We had a fearful time but she recovered.

Ross

I asked God for a sign of His mercy: that she may live. I am very glad he listened… Can you have mercy on me George?

GEORGE

It is Elizabeth's forgiveness you need. Your offence was against her.

Ross

If Valentine… then it is against you as well… I never thought… I never meant…

GEORGE, *interrupting sharply*
> I have determined that we either try to kill each other – and you have a better shot than I do – or we try to reason and possibly reconcile.

After a pause he adds, ironically:
> By the time we have finished this conversation we may find death is the less painful alternative and by far the quicker.

ROSS, *his voice is firmer:*
> A duel is out of the question. The offence is mine. I was enraged with you both and lost control, I took Elizabeth by force. For this I have long felt ashamed I think I always shall. I deeply regret my words and actions of the time.

George, immobile, seems not to have heard him. They both watch the sea in silence for a short while.

GEORGE
> The tide will rises in about one hour or so, I believe.

Anger surged in his voice
> Why do you say I never thought I never meant? Surely you wanted to wreck our marriage. You very nearly achieved it and killed her!

ROSS *in reply, patiently*
> You did say she is out of danger, did you not?

GEORGE
> Yes.

Slowly Ross stands, climbs over the side of the boat, moves towards George and falls onto one knee. Looking at him he opens his hands, palm upwards, one beside the other and says in a determined tone of voice:
ROSS
> I beg your pardon, George.

Taken by surprise GEORGE *looks away in embarrassment and growls:*
> As to forgiveness I believe I am a vindictive type.

ROSS
> You may wish to turn over a new leaf.

Startled George looks him directly in the eyes and slowly heaves himself up, falling onto one knee, facing Ross and opening up his hands towards him just as the other man has done.

GEORGE
I beg your pardon, Ross.

A long silence followed, they continue to sustain each other's gaze until Ross places George's hands as if in prayer and puts his own on either side of them[27]. George looks puzzled, alarmed.

GEORGE
What...?

ROSS
It is about loyalty and protection, an old chivalric gesture. Let us agree that there can be no aggression, no revenge or reprisal as a consequence of our conversation today. This gesture is also about respect for each other. Can we both feel safe here, alone together, so we can both be truthful?

The music ceases. They both stand up together and sit down inside the boat. They are seated side by side, both with strained expressions on their faces. The clamour of the sea-gulls rises sharply.

ROSS *in an even tone of voice, pointedly[28]*
George, what exactly are you asking me to forgive you for?

GEORGE *in his familiar low growl*
Is it a confession you are asking for?

ROSS
A full confession, yes, and for you to be open and honest. I know how startling a request this is, as startling as mine and your demand for forgiveness but I cannot wipe the slate clean unless you convince me that you too are aware of your offences and sincerely regret them[29].

George takes a stick and starts moving it on the ground, shifting pebbles aimlessly,

---

27   This is a central gesture when creating a new knight in chivalry: the feudal Lord takes both hands of the knight (who is kneeling in front of him) enclosing them in his own, as in prayer. The knight thus swears loyalty to the Lord who will protect him. ("Faire obeissance" see Marc Bloch's *Feudal Society*).

28   Unexpectedly Ross takes the initiative leading the exchange in a new direction, he knows that George is in a self-critical mood and his communication confirms this. He continues to be very afraid of George but must now lead the conversation forward.

29   A request for "cards on the table", a clarification on both sides to build trust in their dialogue.

trying to control strong emotions and fighting back tears. The seagulls shriek plunging into the sea[30].

GEORGE

Shall we start at the beginning with Francis?

Ross

Perhaps not I am curious what your wager with Monk may have been. We might start from the end.

GEORGE

The wager… the wager was about Monk seducing Demelza. I'm sorry I threw the money into your face I was trying to make you call another duel: it might have finished you.

Ross

It was Monk who called me out not the other way round.

GEORGE

I had wished he might kill you, I knew he could well achieve it just as I wanted you hanged after Matthew died and our ship was ransacked on this very beach.

GEORGE *seems to be talking about another man, not himself. He wants to get this penance over fast assuming Ross merely wants to humiliate him.*

I paid the witnesses to testify at your trial, I published the libel and had it distributed. Jud was paid to testify against you but did not keep his part of the deal which is why he was later beaten as you suspected. After Monk died I even approached two gentlemen of the law at my club but could not persuade them to bring charges against you for the duel since I could not find anyone to testify that you were at the scene.

Ross

I never saw your look as full of hatred as I did then, George. May I ask why you were or perhaps still are so determined to see me jailed, ruined, dead?

GEORGE

I was Ross, was *(pause)*. Because I am a poisonous, envious snake.

---

30   The music starts again and verbal exchanges take place rapidly.

Tension and the shrieking of seagulls mount.

Ross, *hard hitting but speaking in a quiet voice*
Perhaps more like a poisonous spider tormenting his victims in its web and leaving them half alive waiting in terror for the sting to pierce them. I am thinking of Francis.

GEORGE
There is little kindness in your reply; this is a painful conversation for me as you may imagine. I cannot continue without your help – *the voice breaking* – I am sorry for my actions Ross, I truly am. *George starts playing with the stick again, pushing the pebbles around.*

Ross, *drily*
Concerning Francis, did you really pay him to betray the names of the associates of the Carnmore copper company?

GEORGE
Francis was so angry with you for helping his sister elope that I easily persuaded him to give me the names. I had already offered the payment as an acknowledgement of the losses he sustained playing cards with Cousin Matthew who, as you discovered, was a cheat at cards and fraudulently stripped him of his money. When I hinted to you in the pub that he was paid for the information I was lying, trying to break your friendship. He had by then rejected me and sided with you. It made me feel alone, very lonely (pause) you were right to throw me over the bannister after I'd said it!

He has spoken half-jokingly and they both laugh for a few seconds, this breaks the tension; the birds' dawn chorus takes over from the seagulls.

Ross
I was glad you were not seriously hurt during that fall, I too have suffered from murderous thoughts – *pause* – and I repent – *a long pause* – You may well have wanted to be friends with Francis because your aim was Elizabeth.

GEORGE
I wanted to meet her, yes, but that was not the only reason, I liked him well. I had been his friend since I was a child, as you will remember?

Ross
Did you know that after he quarrelled with you in Bodmin, before my trial,

doctor Enys found him in his room having just tried to shoot himself? He would have been dead but for the gun not firing. Dwight managed to talk sense into him. Just before Francis went down into the mine alone and drowned he revealed to Demelza how he had given you the names of my associates in the copper smelting venture. This enabled you to put financial pressure on most of the shareholders so they withdrew their support. When the venture failed cousin Francis' conscience tormented him with guilt; I presume you know what this word means George. I too liked my cousin well and he understood me. Did you suspect your cousin Matthew of cheating when Francis was ruining himself financially playing cards in your company?[31]

GEORGE

I might have known he was cheating, I was not sure, it was easier to look the other way.

It is very cold but George feels that he is sweating, Ross starts shivering and the seagulls return with loud cries.

ROSS

Did you wish that Francis and myself would be financially ruined so that no one would stand between you and Elizabeth?

GEORGE

For pity's sake do you really have such an appalling opinion of me?

ROSS

I did have George, I did have but I am willing to reconsider… I am assuming you will answer me truthfully: was Francis not caught in a web of mortgages and financial obligations to the Warleggan bank and did you get possession of my promissory note for a thousand pounds with the purpose of asking for immediate repayment which would certainly bankrupt me and land me in a debtor's prison? By chance the fact I had to go and discuss this with Harry Pascoe caused my late homecoming that evening. Had I come home earlier I might have been able to save Francis from drowning. We both tried to hold out and survive somehow but only I was lucky.

GEORGE *is skating on thin ice*

I cannot contradict what you are saying and you know I did nothing illegal.

---

31 The question, unspoken, is: did you drive Francis to his death? The answer comes later with George's letter.

Ross

You will not admit that it was immoral!

GEORGE

Now you are hounding me Ross and you promised respect.

Ross *on a collision course*

The list of the people you hounded and slowly strangled or blackmailed financially till they became your puppets or left the County would take us too long to spell out. The tide is about to come in. Can we agree that having friends is better than being surrounded by dogs on a leash?

GEORGE *in distress*

I will not put up with such insults. Now you are being unfair to me.

Ross, *conciliatory*

If I am I apologise.

GEORGE

You cannot have missed I admit I am at fault. I have been hostile to Demelza and her brothers, I have insulted her to your face, I am sorry for that. She is a wise woman and a faithful wife.

Ross *hard hitting, his voice low*

And you wanted to spoil it for us and hounded her brother Drake.

GEORGE, *bluntly but quietly*

Yes I wanted to spoil what you had, the mine, your wife. You too wanted to spoil my chances with Elizabeth and no holds were barred in that fight. You nearly succeeded.

Ross, *firmly*

In truth at the time I was feeling distraught: the mine was about to close, everything I tried had failed. Elizabeth agreeing to marry you was the last straw. That night I came seeking an explanation, I was beside myself. Her initial replies to me only made matters worse…I lost control, I shall regret it always.

GEORGE, *quietly*

I would not have imagined this attack on Elizabeth from you; I see now why she became hostile to you after we were married.

ROSS

I am not trying to excuse myself; this is a blot on my honour and a stain on my character. I imagine how bitter you must feel. Once again, as you have not so far replied, I beg your forgiveness.

GEORGE

Can you see how fast the tide is flowing? We need to make haste; the waves are coming in[32].

ROSS

The cliffs here are too steep to climb. Let's put the boat out to sea – it will not be easy – and move to the right end of the cove, from there we may climb up.

Ross took an oar and George pushed the boat forward, jumping inside and the took the second oar. They managed with ease to take the boat to the far end of the cove and beached it dragging it up and mooring it. In the process they became rather wet. By now the sun was clearly over the horizon, taking some of the morning chill away. They started climbing the cliff with Ross leading the way and indicating where the path became slippery. On a couple of occasions they steadied each other and once George nearly pulled Ross down with him.

NARRATOR *speaks during their escape from the tide and the climb uphill*

George was mulling over Ross' request for forgiveness in his mind. It pleased him but reconciliation would not alter the "Valentine" problem the two couples were facing. George had started leading the conversation but lost control very quickly, he decided to regain it now. Ross laid ground rules of honesty, respect and compassion and it was surprising how well it worked. Perhaps George would restate them…he had been puzzled when he found Ross praying, (him of all people…) he was afraid, he may have been afraid, indeed he should have been, but he did not behave as if he were frightened. George had certainly prayed when he was afraid Elizabeth may die, it was a normal reaction. George had the thought that God might expect him to forgive Ross and he might find himself unable to do so sincerely. He would be reluctant to fake it. What they had both said about him was sinking in slowly, as if he had picked stinging nettles by mistake and the unpleasant irritation was increasing with a skin rash appearing. He was reminded of how recently he could gladly have killed Ross. There was no one able to hold him to account as Ross had just done and George

---

32   Thus far the bodies have been static, from now on they move and the camera must be more focused on the entire person. The actors could mirror body posture: George following and mirroring Ross, Ross responding with a gesture.

felt almost grateful for it. A response to his request was needed, a refusal would be difficult. Ross had not answered George's request for forgiveness either.

Ross was mentally exhausted, glad George had climbed down yet sad that he himself felt so empty. He had no inclination to forgive George, yet he had to. Reconciliation was only the beginning of a pilgrimage, a long walk of penance for both, with some hope he would in future be able to forgive George in his heart and George forgive him likewise. The thought that he himself might not be willing or able to accept forgiveness (assuming George was prepared to offer it) came to him. He had begged for a pardon (well he could hardly have said anything else) but was he prepared to receive it?

End NARRATOR *voice*

Having reached a safe ledge on the cliff they sat down side by side looking out to the sea. The powerful Atlantic tide was in full strength, the birds were singing.

Ross *breaks the silence*

George, had you wished to do away with me you just missed a great opportunity **to push me off the cliff!**

GEORGE

You likewise had several chances to hold my head underwater and escape scot-free! **Ross, am I forgiven?**

Ross

Yes, today I can start to forgive you. And is Ross forgiven…?

The wait seemed a very long time.
George took Ross' hands, joined them and held them together in his, just as Ross had done with him earlier.

GEORGE

It is a pledge, is it not? God our Father forgive us, as we forgive each other. We have nursed hatred in our heart and done what is wrong in your eyes, as we humbly confessed. Lord give us wisdom, strength and sincere repentance. Teach us how to forgive.

Ross

Amen.

There was nothing left to say. They sat in silence a while longer, George had left his horse tethered near the house. They walked towards it and parted, shaking hands for the first time in years. Ross walked slowly to his door[33].

1e   Int. Nampara's breakfast room Day
Ross, Demelza, Dwight

Nampara: Ross and Demelza are having breakfast in silence, enter Dwight.

DWIGHT
> Ross, Elizabeth is out of danger, she is so much better, a sign of God's blessing.

ROSS
> I know, I was on the beach. I watched the sun rise with George. We had a serious talk, forgave each other and were reconciled...When Elizabeth is quite recovered I must have a talk with her too.

DWIGHT *murmurs as if to himself*
> It was bravely done.

ROSS
> You know I am unbelievably tired, I need to sleep.

DWIGHT
> And you are very wet!

ROSS
> The tide caught up with us and washed our sins away.

Cut to Demelza tidying up the breakfast table with a worried look on her face[34].

---

33   A long silence, the music plays an important role, alternatively one could attempt to create real silence, with just nature's sounds in the background.

34   Relief, astonishment, fatigue and concern for the future blend in this compact scene.

Act 2[35]

2a   Int. Bedroom at Trentwith Day
George, Elizabeth, Ursula

Camera starts on gentle snowfall

NARRATOR

Snow started slowly in the evening, by morning two inches lay on the ground and icicles covered trees and bushes. Looking out of the window Elizabeth recalled playing snowballs in this garden with the Poldark cousins. George came to inquire whether she had slept well and picked up the child from the cot. His attentions after she had been so ill were increasingly warm, his pleasure in the little bear – as he called her – Ursula, evident.

GEORGE

I shall not be able to go to Truro today, I'll enjoy being with my little girl and her beautiful mother

ELIZABETH

Careful how you hold her head, *(George, feeling criticized, hesitates)* I trust you with her, but she is so tiny.

GEORGE *sarcastic*

Well she is premature.

ELIZABETH

Do you remember playing snowballs in the garden with Francis and myself?

GEORGE

Yes, with Ross too: I remember how I felt trapped in a corner, hurt by their rebuffs. I vowed when I grew up I would never again be lonely, feeling left out and socially awkward.

---

35   *Be still my soul* thy God doth undertake
to guide the future as he hath the past
Thy hope, thy confidence let nothing shake (on Sibelius Finland tune)

ELIZABETH

Childhood memories are often distorted you know, I do not recall you being ignored by the cousins.

GEORGE

That is how it felt. I hated myself for being so meek and pliant, planning revenge even then. My politeness was a studied sham. *Ursula opens and closes her eyes as if in a dream, he kisses her cheek and carefully lays her down.*

GEORGE

Elizabeth, these days I have been worried for you.

ELIZABETH

I feel so much better, rest assured.

GEORGE

I was concerned that I had been so angry and critical. You felt unable to confide in me and did something very silly and dangerous taking that potion. You could both have died.

Elizabeth is startled and is about to answer, GEORGE's *voice hardens with anger and anxiety:*

Do not try to hide or deny it, both doctors were present and have agreed on this: had they not found an antidote you would have died. The potion deranged your mind you became delirious and revealed what you tried so hard to conceal: that Ross, before we married, early in May, had taken you by force. The wording of your oath to me, that you had given yourself willingly only to Francis and myself, suddenly made sense. You had not given yourself to Ross, but there is a possibility that on that night Valentine may have been conceived.

He pauses, sits by her, takes her hand and kisses it:

My angel you ought not to have lied to me.

ELIZABETH *blushes*

What will you think of me now? I was scared of your anger, your jealousy, scared for Valentine.

GEORGE *pretending to be angry*

And for Ross too, I imagine. *(Pause)* I may be forced to call Ross out. It is forbidden, I know, a duel is risky. I wish to avenge you, I want him punished. What do you think?!

ELIZABETH *confused, concerned*

I have lost one husband shall I lose another? Is it really for me that you desire to call him out or are you moved by the old enmity? I know him well: he is punished by his own guilt.

GEORGE *with curiosity*

Did he apologise to you himself, when?

ELIZABETH

Your jealousy! Will it ever cease? How could I have spoken to him after I married you? No, he did not apologise, he is too proud to say it but he knows he wronged me. We were friends and sweethearts a long time ago before he went into the army. We considered ourselves engaged, I was only sixteen. I thought him dead when I agreed to marry Francis but I soon realised what a mistake I had made.

GEORGE

Did you imagine going back to Ross after you were disappointed by Francis? Perhaps you are trying to spare my feelings or avoid my jealousy.

ELIZABETH *soothingly*

George, one's first love is never forgotten, like a pleasant dream, a distant memory. His friendship and his help with financial matters were an anchor for me after Francis died. Now I am your wife. You have my trust, loyalty and affection. If you cannot see that or you cannot accept Valentine our marriage has no future.

GEORGE *turning to the window and moving away from her to hide his agitation*

I want to be a father to Valentine but I need to know you can accept your husband as the man he is now and help him become the man he ought to be: kinder and sincere.

ELIZABETH *softly and moving closer*

This is my duty as your wife: have I failed you?

GEORGE

I know I have a dutiful wife; when we married you implied your respect for me was greater than your affection. I recall saying that love might come later. Can happiness grow like a new shoot from a tree scarred by lightening? Can it dispel our present loneliness and fear?

ELIZABETH

You know Ross means nothing to me now, he is happily married – *her voice rises in anger* – I do not wish to speak to him ever again. He posed as a friend, then betrayed my trust and hurt me deeply. I did not know what to do for the best. When you became so distant and neglectful of myself and Valentine I felt abandoned, weak and vulnerable.

GEORGE

I am a better man than I was. I can see now the shadows in my soul, the jealousy in my heart, the arrogance of my attitude. When Ross asked for my forgiveness I knew I had to do the same. We both asked for and received compassion. At first it was hard but in the end it became easy and a great relief. The bitterness and hostility are gone; we can now breathe freely talking to each other. What has happened must remain hidden; we have to deal with our feelings about it as best we can. I even hope we might be friends in future.

ELIZABETH *in disbelief*

George, I fear this is just a dream and I shall awake to find you unchanged.

She picks up the whimpering baby knowing the contact will give her comfort; she is sweating and trembling still waiting for George's rage to explode.

He smiles – **smiles!** *– George spoke haltingly as if his throat hurt:*

GEORGE

I know you are blameless I shan't ask you any questions on this painful event. Ursula is our child, Valentine was born to you: you are both dear to me. I shall be a good father and make up to him for the past, this is the only way. I feel wounded of course but you'll help me keep this promise.
She is relieved hearing the strength of his resolve, he continues steadily:
I am holding fast to the pledge I made on the night you nearly died, the promise I made to God and myself that if you lived I would change my ways. I gladly forgive you for taking the potion and trying to deceive me and I hope you have forgiven the unhappiness caused by my jealousy.
She was starting to feel safe now, he gently kissed her hand.

ELIZABETH

I procured the potion in London when your suspicion and hostility grew stronger; I only decided to take it after that dreadful evening when you came home unexpectedly. After Morwenna told you she was marrying Drake and you threw her out of our home.

GEORGE *apologetic*

I shall never again behave as I did then. We should ask to see them together and, with your help, I'll apologize to both. While we are on the subject of apologies: Ross wishes to make his regret clear to you.

ELIZABETH *vehemently*

I do not wish to speak to him, nor do I intend to forgive him.

GEORGE

When he spoke to me he seemed racked with remorse. Will you not listen to what he has to say?

ELIZABETH *bitterly*

It has taken him all these years to express his regret. Perhaps he is merely sorry he was unmasked.

GEORGE

Even with your help, Elizabeth, it will still take me many years to change yet I tell you I am glad I can drop the mask with you. This is, truly, the man you married. Will you stand by him?

ELIZABETH

For the courage of this admission I respect you all the more.
She kisses him lightly on the cheek and thinks their life together has been blessed with a second chance. George grins, puts his hand in a pocket and takes out pearl earrings which he fastens on her ears. She looks in the mirror and sees a future, a possible happiness, a kinder, more tolerant George. Her embrace and their kiss become passionate.

2b   Ext. on horseback, countryside (winter scene) Day
Ross, Dwight

DWIGHT

Glad to meet you Ross, I was on my way home to a warm glass of wine.

ROSS

Is Caroline keeping well?

DWIGHT

Yes and so is your family I trust. You do not look cheerful though.

Ross

I need a friend a good friend like you. Can we stay here a while: I do not want our conversation overheard.

They both dismount and sit on the trunk of a fallen tree, in a space under a big oak (or they keep riding slowly side by side).

Ross

I am on my way home from meeting Elizabeth at Trentwith. She is adamant she will not forgive me. She suggests I was sorry I have been unmasked rather than repentant. She even said I was inclined to excuse my action, I only regretted the unforeseen consequence and I am feeling ashamed rather than guilty. She argued I always made my own rules and I did not bend to laws or commandments; she did not wish to encourage this attitude by condoning what I did to her. She said she would pray God to give me sincere remorse. She hoped I would learn to obey and stop seeing myself as superior to lesser mortals and their petty justice. I explained again that her hesitation and mixed messages over the years, her betrayal of myself and of Francis (as I saw it on that night) in agreeing to marry George were partly to blame for my feeling beside myself and acting wildly. On this she did not contradict me.

I think she is being unjust and vindictive, I understand she may not wish to forgive me but she need not indulge in reprimanding me.

I listened and tried to counter her statements but to no avail. I felt she wanted to punish me, I perceived she had a right to do so. I am annoyed with her and with myself. We simply talked at cross purposes yet we used to understand one another so well.

After a short silence Dwight *replied:*

I'd like to understand the point she is making as you say she knows you well. She is, I suppose, the victim. We must listen to her carefully. I am not saying she is right but we should try to consider her statement seriously. She is making an allegation, framing your action as a refusal of discipline and she says you justify yourself by your libertine[36] ideas. She is pointing to an attitude rather than a single episode of loss of control. Is there any truth in her statement that you only admitted your responsibility because it became unavoidable, and that up to now you had justified or at least excused yourself and felt no need to try to remedy or apologize?

---

36   The meaning of "libertine" in the eighteenth century did not have solely the modern sexual connotation. It pointed to a rebellious, anti-religious attitude; the word suggests a misuse of freedom.

Ross

There were some extenuating circumstances which I mentioned to George adding that I did not wish to make excuses for myself. I am in the wrong.

Dwight

You are the person who decides what the rules are and what the consequences being judge and jury.

Ross

You could say that, since I have long been an atheist and will not accept impositions from a debased, perverted church, but my rules are not self-serving, far from it; I am a severe judge of my actions. I bear my guilt and suffer the consequences of my sins.

Dwight

Elizabeth may have a point after all. Your position has a drawback: you cannot offer forgiveness to yourself, not even after making amends. You cannot change your rules. Mercy can only come from another human being.

Ross

After our meeting that cursed night I suppressed the guilt I was feeling, it was a dead end, I could not change the past and after her marriage I could not even talk to her. I was unaware that she may have been left with child. Regarding what happened on the night my self-criticism was useless self-torture.

Dwight

And you wish to keep on a path which you name a dead end street, correct? *There was a silence as Ross understood Dwight was asking a critical question. His shoulders hunched and his gaze lowered, he replied:*

Ross

I felt trapped.

Dwight

I hear you say you are free and master of yourself. Could it be the other way round: the self is the master, law giver and inflexible judge?

As Dwight voice was gaining strength Ross' shoulders sank even further.

Ross

I may be totally deceiving myself. Can you help me discern an inner voice born from heart and reason, guided by experience?

DWIGHT

Can you accept there is an authority outside your "self" held by others who can pass judgement, punish and forgive? There is religion's fallible reading of God's words; there are opinions of respected friends, moral philosophers and familiar voices: listen to those. Are there friends whose ruling you are willing to surrender to? How does it feel to surrender freedom, this freedom to remain unforgiven? Is the taste of the apple in the Garden of Eden so enticing? "You shall know good from evil the snake said to Eve in the garden and you shall be like Gods".

ROSS

I do not wish to be like God, I do not even believe God exists!
The tone of voice hinted at his frustration.

DWIGHT

What one believes often depends on what one does. Can you let this Other spell your responsibility, judge and forgive you? If today you hear God's call listen to His voice, you may find He exists. You may not like what you hear and refuse to listen but He will stand at your door and call on you again.

ROSS

When I have hoped for a merciful God I have found the Satan: the inhuman judges, the merciless punishment of poor devils, sadistic clerics. I know, I can go to the book of the Bible but I am alone with it. The Psalm "Have mercy on me, Lord, according to thy loving kindness"… spoke to me, a man to another man, separated by more than two thousand years. Can't you understand? When I find myself in a spiritual desert (it has happened) I am likely to find Satan, not God. His accusations against me, my failings act like a barrier. If I could remove this anger against myself and my rage against this unjust world, this pitiless Christian church I may break free. George has less of a hurdle: his conscience is weak, he approves the ways of this world and this church or perhaps God has decided to accept his prayer and not mine, for his own reasons. I am tied by my own character and moral feelings: I have often seen myself as a good Samaritan. When I saved Demelza from the beatings and the poverty I was later well rewarded. When I have been kind I have felt good about myself. Life seldom punished me when I did something I disapproved of. (*pause*)
George's transformation is a wonder. Why does God not visit me with a miracle, an angel, anything?
The irritation in his voice is mounting, the conversation is treading on water. Many old spiritual wounds are revisited.

DWIGHT

By paying attention to yourself, considering what your condition is or should be, what you are supposed to do to satisfy God you are losing track of him. When you see Christ in the desert keep him in your sight, forgetting everything else[37].

ROSS

What if it is Satan and not God? I am coming to the conclusion they live in close proximity, I need keep my wits about me in the wilderness (a long pause) We shall continue this discussion. I bid you good day.

Ross, somewhat irritably, goes to his horse and unties it, mounts and heads towards home, as does Dwight. (If they have been proceeding slowly on horseback they separate quickly).

2c Evensong[38] Ext. & Church Int. Day
Ross, George, their families, Rev. Odgers and his congregation

The two families meet outside the church before Evensong: George and Elizabeth with Valentine and Geoffrey Charles, Ross with Clowance in his arms and Demelza with Jeremy. They exchange knowing glances and enter the church. The service starts: Rev. Odgers enters and goes to the altar flanked by the sexton and his son. The church is half empty and each family takes its usual place: the Warleggans in the front row on one side, Ross and his family on the third row, on the other side. They are in full view of each other and stand as the Vicar approaches the altar.

ODGERS

Peace be with you.

CONGREGATION

And with thy spirit.

Text of the general confession[39]:

---

37   D. Bonhoeffer: "Faith means to find, hold to and cast my anchor on a foundation outside myself, on an eternal foundation, on Christ. Faith means to be captivated by the gaze of Jesus Christ; ... Faith means to be *torn out of imprisonment in one's own ego*". *Ethics* (p.147; publ. 1998, written 1940 to 1943).

38   One might use Sibelius' Finland music to which the hymn *stand firm my soul* is sang.

39   Taken from a leaflet in York's Minster. A beautiful prayer which is quoted (in the novel Demelza Poldark) by Demelza "I followed the devices and the desires of my heart".

Almighty and most merciful Father; we have erred, and strayed from thy ways like lost sheep. We have followed too much the devices and desires of our own hearts. We have offended against thy holy laws. We have left undone those things which we ought to have done; and we have done those things which we ought not to have done; and there is no health in us. But Thou, O Lord, have mercy upon us, miserable offenders. Spare Thou them, O God, which confess their faults. Restore Thou them that are penitent; according to thy promises declared unto mankind in Christ Jesus our Lord. And grant, O most merciful Father, for his sake, that we may hereafter live a godly, righteous and sober life, to the glory of thy holy Name. Amen.

The minister pronounces the absolution

Odgers starts the general confession too fast and muttering (although it is supposed to be read with the congregation kneeling here everybody is standing). Directing his peculiarly blue eyes to George and Elizabeth Ross slowly goes on his knees, with Demelza holding his hand. George, after a moment of surprise does the same, and they both bow their head. Some people in the church, uncertain about what to do, also fall on their knees but some do not. Odgers notices and intones the rest of the confession with feeling and slow solemnity. Then follows the communal recital of Our Father (all standing) with voices gaining in strength (George and Ross and both wives again exchanging friendly smiles) and growing to a solemn finale: For thine is the Kingdom, the power and the glory...
The rest of evensong is omitted, the next scene sees Odgers walking towards the entrance porch, after the end of the service. The rest of the congregation is exiting, turning their backs to the two families who are moving from the pews towards each other in the central corridor.
Demelza curtsies, looking first at Elizabeth, then at Valentine. Elizabeth gestures agreement with her head and Demelza picks Valentine up (Ross has in the meantime picked Clowance up, she is hugging him partly hiding his face).

ELIZABETH
Valentine, this is Aunt Demelza.

DEMELZA *indicating Ross to Valentine:*
This is uncle Ross with our little Clowance, she is a little younger than you are.

They find themselves together outside the entrance and greet Rev. Odgers briefly. Geoffrey Charles happily greets Ross and Demelza, Elizabeth moves closer and greets Demelza warmly.

ELIZABETH

Dear Demelza how your Jeremy has grown! Is he pleased with his sister?

DEMELZA

Yes they play well together. Yesterday he made a little snowman, they were disappointed when it melted.

Elizabeth is monitoring George out of the corner of her eye and waiting for Ross to emerge from the porch, Ross salutes George politely, carefully, to the amazement of all the people now outside the church. Elizabeth catches his eye and he approaches them.

ELIZABETH

George, Demelza tells me her children made a snowman; I was imagining one in our garden as well; (*she spoke slowly, tentatively and seductively*) sometime soon we could invite her and the children for the afternoon; If the weather is mild the children can play outside (*she adds looking at him*) if you feel it is appropriate.

GEORGE

When would you suggest?

ELIZABETH

Tomorrow, if it is convenient.

DEMELZA *turned to Ross*

You are in Truro tomorrow I believe.

ROSS

I was planning to go but there have been problems at the mine, I can go later in the week.

George watched the negotiation thinking Ross had never visited their Trentwith home in amity after their marriage.

GEORGE

Well (*slowly turning to Ross*) if your business at the mine is finished you could come at the end of the afternoon and take your family home. I shall work in my study and inspect the snowman.

The joke did not quite break the tension.

Bravely GEOFFREY CHARLES *intervened*

What a good idea uncle George I'll throw snowballs at my cousins!

ELIZABETH
You'll do nothing of the sort, they are too young!

DEMELZA *feels the impulse to flee but manages to say*
I am truly pleased and thank you for the invitation. We'll come tomorrow after lunch then, and return home before dinner. I am obliged to you and George for your kindness.

ROSS *politely, thinking there would be talk of nothing else in the village*
I thank you too.

Everyone beamed, colluding in this stilted social performance[40].
When each family turns slowly towards home seemingly in concentration, hiding the desire to escape the universal curiosity Demelza feels a secret joy and George notices the harmonious stillness of the winter landscape.
The Poldark couple walks arm in arm, Jeremy skipping by their side.

A little later ROSS *observes*
Alea iacta est, the only bit of Latin I remember: it means the deed is done the dice is thrown. Elizabeth must be in agreement with George. Even if she will not forgive me they want us to be good neighbours. Now it is up to you to re-new your friendship with Elizabeth. What each one of us knows is knowledge shared, we are working together to hide this secret like the silent snow covers footfalls.

DEMELZA
Really, Ross, I did not know the story in full till Dwight mentioned a small detail to me. I am not surprised she will not forgive you.

There was both criticism and complicity in her voice, her tone subdued.

ROSS *self-deprecatingly*
Truth will out, its voice is small but obstinate. I could not be completely honest knowing you'd take her side.

---

40 Everybody's gaze creates a fishbowl effect around them; they are watching themselves and are being watched.

She looks at him and presses her hand on his arm, with sympathy.
A Link scene could show the three children playing in the snow.

NARRATOR

A streetwise and resolute Demelza befriends the delicately aristocratic Elizabeth: they maintain an emotional distance but are able to assist each other, this lessens Elizabeth's painful sense of loneliness.

Ross continues to battle with himself watching George warily: he knows he is in danger of losing his emotional control. He is still suspicious of George's motives, at times unable or unwilling to believe his sincerity or the stability of the changes he has witnessed in him. This different George, uncertain like a man who feels lost and his reliance on Ross' support fascinates and alarms him. He occasionally feels furious, has the impulse to slam George down severely on account of the past and he keeps reminding himself he has forgiven George or is trying to. The question Dwight has posed occupies his thoughts: is he defending his soul, his values, his freedom of choice or covering up self-serving bias?

The families have met twice, Ross keeping aloof from Elizabeth. Cautious politeness prevails edging around awkward topics. Demelza has gradually become more confident threading the minefields of befriending Elizabeth and helping their children mix. She has been practicing some Christmas Carols with Elizabeth on a spinet, leading the children in a carol his brother Sam had taught her. George seldom emerges from the study, when she met him he is always welcoming in his formal manner.

One day Ross came by to take the family home; he was waiting for the end of singing practice and went to greet George, who had been musing over their recent meeting at the beach. George showed him into the study, through the parlour where their physical fight had taken place four years earlier.

NARRATOR *ends*

2d   Int. Trentwith study Afternoon
George, Ross, Demelza

Camera has followed George showing Ross into the parlour, dialogue starts abruptly. Emotions and exchanges become raw threading a slippery path.

GEORGE

If I may ask why did you decide to kneel at Evensong?

Ross

On impulse, thinking I was the lost sheep mentioned, but God was still abroad.

GEORGE, *caution and formality melted away*
I still do not understand how you could forgive me I do not think I deserved it. Somehow I expected you to trust me.

ROSS *taken by surprise cannot master his temper*
Why? No, you did not deserve it. Try remember this: I gave you credit. If I had not forgiven you how could we deal with this utter tangle, this mess: what I did, what you did and the consequences? You saw it clearly: the alternative was between killing the other or forgiving, talking with sincerity and being reconciled.

GEORGE, *reflectively, as if talking to himself*
It is alive in my memory: I often remember that moment on the beach, going down on my knees and I know it might happen again if I make similar mistakes. It is hard to carry the guilt I am feeling, even harder to imagine failing again.

ROSS *losing his patience at the wrong moment:*
Stop whining, this is exactly where I believe you should be!

GEORGE
I am not whining, I am asking for your help by spelling out my fears. Do not crush me.

ROSS *circles around the room, then speaks looking out of the study's window.*
I am unkind because I am unable to keep my anger with you in check. It is high time I learned to master myself.

GEORGE *silently accepts this apology and continues*
Tell me what you think I should do… Help me!

ROSS *having regained his poise:*
We hold on to the forgiveness, not only for the past but for the present: rifts and resentment were not magically healed. I am, as I hope you are, ready to forgive you today without hostility, if I am able to check my anger. Your anger with yourself also needs to be restrained: remain confident you are in control and able to see and remedy mistakes. It is a very uncomfortable ride for both; it may continue for some time. It will hurt: a reminder that we have hurt other people. I have seen your progress; I trust and hope your change is taking roots but we must both be patient and take our medicine. I see your good will, your resolve; I'll continue to help and be lenient. I know you could have been a great deal harder on me.

GEORGE, *distressed*

The survival of my marriage depends on breaking my heart of stone and putting a human heart in its place. For Elizabeth I know I am willing to do it. Can it be done? *A pause, then as if speaking to himself:* I overheard Demelza saying to Elizabeth: "At first, irrationally, I could not help blaming Julia's death on you[41]... and now you have blue eyed Valentine"[42].

Ross *suddenly blushes*

Little as I believe in God I sometimes pray for mercy. What you've just said is a hard blow to me, George.

GEORGE

It is as hard on me as it is on you. I would be glad to know you pray a little for me as well.

Ross *adds quietly*

May I ask how Valentine fares with you these days?

GEORGE

I treat him as a good father should, or, at least, I wear a credible mask for a six-year-old. I have even apologised to him (in words a child can understand) for my past rejections: you should have seen how alarmed he looked at first...! He is smart, attractive, (*a tease creeps into his voice*) may be a little strong headed. I can bond with him again, I must. Elizabeth expects no less. And she'll be watching. (*His tone from reflective becomes ironically formal*).
Is this a satisfactory answer to your question?

Ross

Indeed it is.

GEORGE

We are all bearing your sin together, even Valentine, the only innocent one. You are looking in the mirror of your own conscience but you do not stand alone.

Ross

Neither do you, George, stand alone with your remorse. We are asking for

---

41   Demelza and Ross' first child Julia died because both she and mother were infected with a respiratory illness after Demelza spent some time looking after Geoffrey Charles, Elizabeth's first born, when the entire household of Francis Poldark had the infectious illness.

42   A discreet suggestion that she knows Valentine may be Ross' child.

God's help: one prays for the other, not solely in words but in action, in kindness and in comforting *(Ross moves closer to George)*. How am I to answer the distress signal you are sending out? Am I permitted to come closer, meet you behind the polite mask?

George moves away, towards the drinks cabinet.
GEORGE
Which one would you like?

Ross
Geneva if you please.

Silently George fills two glasses, offers him one and sits down, some distance away.

Demelza's singing accompanied by the spinet can be heard: the first lines of Hark, the herald Angels sing[43], her voice rising louder then falling silent. A thin voice, Valentine's, then Jeremy's, take up the song and their voices rise together. Elizabeth is accompanying them on the spinet. Silent tears are falling down George's face; sipping his drink he seems unaware of them. Ross, acutely embarrassed, tries not to look in his direction and is wondering how to respond. The singing is filling the house with music, when it stops
GEORGE *asks, casually*
The ten pounds I threw back in your face in London, did I ever explain…?

Ross
I could easily guess, and, yes, you did briefly explain when we were in the cove.

GEORGE
Did you explain those events to Demelza?

Ross *smiles to himself.*
Not this detail, George. Demelza might get really angry and a pretty temper she has…

GEORGE
Why are you shielding me?

---

43   Wesley, 1737. "Hark the herald angels sing 'Glory to the new born King. Peace on earth and mercy mild, God and sinners reconciled' Joyful all ye nation rise, join the triumph of the skies, with angelic host proclaim 'Christ is born in Bethlehem. Hark the herald Angels sing Glory to the new born King'". This is the same carol George shall later hear sung in the Chapel; it has a warm, fast rhythm.

Ross

I am protecting myself. In this unholy mess your wager daring Monk to seduce Demelza is just a detail

GEORGE

Not really. Beyond the seduction I knew this may lead to a duel and your killing, it nearly did.

Ross, *drily*

Yes, I narrowly avoided losing one arm, now I am fully recovered.

GEORGE *had stopped crying and looked pale*

Wouldn't this world be a better place without me?

Ross

You have gained my respect and my trust George. Now you speak like a weakling, you talk of giving up.

Ross, standing quite some distance away has awakened to the seriousness of George's statement and is looking straight at him.

GEORGE

Even snakes, behind the mask, have a *conscience whose bite is toothless*[44].

Ross

Behind the mask is there a man I could talk to?

GEORGE

Yes, but the man is behind a bolted door in arrogant solitude and he is crying. You could break down the door if you wanted to.

Ross

I would be disrespectful towards you if I forced my entry; try unlocking the door and opening up.

Ross had come closer and put his hand on George's shoulder but George had moved away awkwardly, then he spoke slowly in a flat tone:

---

44 This means his conscience is reproaching him (bite) but it is unable to force him to change (toothless).

GEORGE

You will be walking home with Demelza I imagine. May I come along with both of you? A pretty temper she has, you said?

Ross *unhappy at this prospect*

Come to us, let me know when you wish to. In my library a talk can be kept private. Consider if you really need to talk to Demelza of what passed in London. It caused a strain in our marriage. I believe some details are best left unsaid; you and I know at present what we need to know.

GEORGE

I and my snake's conscience believe otherwise…another drink and I may just manage this confession. May I accompany you home?

Ross

Should I speak to her first?

GEORGE

You are still trying to shield me. I shall not hide any longer. From this day onwards I shall not lie, dissemble or manipulate, **however frightened and ashamed I may be of the truth: you see that I am**!

Ross takes hold of George's broad shoulders in a firm grip and draws him close to his chest. George buries his face in Ross' shoulder, trembling slightly. They remain in that posture for a full minute until George stops shaking and gazes into Ross' eyes.

GEORGE

I thank you *(then moves away to sit in an armchair, close to his drink)*.

Ross *sits down beside him*

My privilege.

After a guilty plea comes judgment, poor human justice pronounced by one sinner on another. If your words speak the truth they come from the heart and God alone can judge you, knowing your sincerity and your sin better than you yourself do.

Receiving his mercy, you stand before his justice, they are one and the same. When truth shall flower on earth and justice rain down from heaven justice and peace shall meet. In place of despair receive hope. Accept whatever sentence will be spoken within you, embrace what God or life will send you, break away from barren guilt.

I too have travelled the road of repentance and I travelled it on my own. I have seen rivers appear in dry land, the sand covered with spring flowers, the gifts of a rich season of fruits where I expected dryness and thirst[45].

GEORGE *was lost in his thoughts and may not have been listening*
I can't do this without your help Ross, I can't. Do you still hate me?

Ross (*Ross's voice had an icy edge*)
Yes, sometimes but the feeling is less intense and less frequent. Memories of my anger are reminders of my own offence and a humbling evidence of my lack of generosity. As I try to fight this hatred down I confess how deeply I allowed it to take root in my soul. *He falters, swallowing hard. George lifts his head and takes Ross' hand in his own.*

GEORGE
May your heart also find peace. *(Ross remains silent).*
I am trying to accept Gods judgement on my life, asking him to shatter my arrogance… *(Ross interrupts him in an angry voice).*

Ross
God help me subdue mine arrogance, so different from yours… yet equally strong. I regret the violence, in words and deeds I have offered. You were abusing me but this will not justify my reaction. I wish to say how much I regret hurting you in the past and tell you it will not happen in future. Even if we may be in conflict it must be resolved peacefully.

GEORGE
You, Ross have shown me how to acknowledge my past failings with dignity, keep my self-respect when begging forgiveness. Begging because I need to be forgiven but I do not deserve it as yet. A few weeks ago this would have been impossible for me. Your example made it feasible, reasonable and almost easy. *(George looks down at his hands)* Then I had no choice but to kneel, listen and remain silent as I cannot make any excuses for my… For mine…

Noises in the house move closer and Demelza knocks at the door, opens it, fully dressed, ready to leave. Gaily she says:
DEMELZA
A very enjoyable singing practice! *She stops, looks around, senses the tension, turns*

---

45   A personal rendering of quotations from Psalms and from Isaiah 35, 6-7. I think we must in a contemporary rendering go back to the biblical language of God's mercy, justice and powerful salvation, *not abandon its riches to Bible belt fanatics.*

to George, If it is in order we shall go home Ross.

Ross

Sometime George wishes to see our new library *(turning to George)* Let us know when you may be able to come to Nampara.

GEORGE

The present time is a good one if it suits you, if Demelza agrees.

DEMELZA

When we arrive home it will be tea and bedtime for the children, I need to see to them, Ross can show you the library.

Ross

I'd rather spend time with the children: you may be the hostess.

DEMELZA *puzzled*

I am happy to be guided by your wishes.

Cut (from behind) to the three adults walking down the road, Jeremy alongside[46].

2e   Int. Nampara's sitting room lit by candles[47], evening
Ross, George, Demelza.

Ross comes into the room from the stairs. Demelza, with George after her, enters the room from the library door, both with sober faces. George makes a brief bow and speaks in a detached tone.

GEORGE

I'll take my leave, I am greatly in your debt. *(Ross tries to reach for his hand but he shakes his head)* I really need to go home it is a little late: Demelza can tell you of our conversation I thank you both.

He is barely in control of himself as he leaves. Demelza collapses onto the sofa.

---

46   Camera filming from increasing distance before fade out.

47   Candles may give a shade of unreality to the room, what follows has a fairy tale feel.

DEMELZA

It is the strain let me rest. Are the children...?

ROSS

Settled yes, now I need to settle my wife. *(Ross is holding her, with increasingly sexual undertones. She responds for a while then suddenly she starts to weep, Ross gently helps her to stand up and moves with her towards the stairs)* Time for bed!

2f NARRATOR   Ext., Path to Trentwith Late evening
George, later Drake, Sam, Morwenna,
the Methodist congregation

NARRATOR

The cold wind helps George calm down and gather his ideas. He is riding his horse onto the path towards Trentwith, longing to meet Elizabeth and unable to explain why he feels so relieved. His determination to submit had been inflexible. Hearing himself admit his wrongdoings aloud to this woman had been close to unbearable but now it was over and Demelza had welcomed him. Initially, when they entered the library there had been a tingle of excitement and expectation with tacit acknowledgement on both sides of the true purpose of the visit. She struggled at first after he spelled out tactfully that the wager between himself and Monk (of which she clearly knew nothing) was on whether Monk would be able to seduce her. Shock flashed across her face; he waited in silence until she had composed herself and fiercely criticized him. He had seen it coming and had time to prepare for impact. He remained silent until he felt able to respond. He could make no excuse for his actions, he said, except that he had been beside himself with suspicion and jealousy of Ross. He had hoped Monk may kill Ross. He then told her Drake's persecution was partly due to his befriending Geoffrey Charles and partly to his being her brother but after Drake had spoken to Elisabeth she requested it be stopped and George complied. Demelza had replied, sharply, she hoped he might be able to speak to Drake, soon

After a long silence George asks if there is anything else she desires to ask or tell him. In an anguished voice (DEMELZA's voice here) she replies:

"Are you now regretting your attempts to hurt and destroy two people close and very dear to me? Insults to myself I can easily forgive. Shall we continue to fear you or have your heart and your purpose so altered that we can now trust you?"

Silence, again. He begs her to trust the sincerity of his repentance, of his wish to make amends.

George slowly goes down onto one knee. Can he hope she may forgive him? He waits, she composes herself again. Demelza says she is very happy reconciliation has taken place between the two families, particularly between him and Ross. She bears him no ill will. She hopes past bitterness will soon be forgotten. She praises George's moral courage. She silently raises him and gives him her hand, which George holds for a moment. It is warm and her palm is perspiring. He senses how distressed she is.

NARRATOR *stops*

As the narrator relates what has happened the horse with his master are progressing carefully along the path lit by a full moon. They come up to the Chapel where a service is drawing to a close. People are singing "Hark the Herald Angels sing". On impulse he draws near and dismounts, walking to the threshold and moving just inside the door, ready to leave at the end of the carol. Drake comes to offer him a prayer book. In the dim light they only identify each other when Drake is quite close. The singing of the carol continues. Now the narrator has finished and the action is slowed by the camera.

They stand gazing at each other and GEORGE *murmurs*:
    I am asking your forgiveness, Drake.

He *then falls slowly onto one knee and is immediately raised by* DRAKE *who looks at him saying:*
    As Christ forgave me I forgive you[48].

At this point Morwenna turns her head round, and sees George tentatively offering his hand to Drake who takes it with a slight bow George nods in reply and leaves.
Only Sam, the preacher and Drake's brother, who is facing the Congregation has seen what happened. He speaks to the small Methodist community:
SAM
    Let me say a word about reconciliation and forgiveness. If there be a quarrel or anger within your family or with your neighbour God wants each one of us this Christmas to make peace. Peace on this earth. He wants you to do this today, now. We thank the Lord of Peace for his blessing today. May God protect this community holding us in the hollow of his hand.

CONGREGATION
    Amen[49].

---

48   A short scene, both showing surprise.
49   Cut to George now approaching Trentwith's gate.

2g Int. Trentwith Hall
George and Elisabeth

George sees Elizabeth sitting by the fire, her eyes closed and the sewing on her laps. His long kiss surprises her. He holds her with protective tenderness, a smile spreads from his eyes and lights up his face. She feels safe, wrapped by his body and his gaze.

There could be a longer love scene later in the bedroom but I think it should stop early, Elizabeth may gently decline. There may be a little later a longer lovemaking scene of Ross and Demelza (the sexual tension between them having started to build up earlier, at the end of 2e). Slow down the build-up of foreplay and move ahead (implying rather than showing the orgasmic moments) to show the relaxation after sex and the couple's tenderness.

2h Int. Bedroom at Nampara Night
Ross and Demelza

Demelza late at night is putting out the fire in the fireplace, before going to bed (or they may be talking to each other in bed relaxing after making love).

DEMELZA

Ross how do you understand what is happening with us, George and Elizabeth? She has asked me to go with her to speak to Morwenna tomorrow. I feel I am riding a horse picking up speed, knowing it may bolt or run away yet I cannot dismount. We risk reopening old wounds with Morwenna and Drake, memories of her late husband's unfeeling cruelty.

ROSS

As you say we must ride it out now even as it is picking up speed dangerously. How could this meeting of George and Drake ever happen? Why did he even enter the building? What is George now thinking and feeling?

DEMELZA

I think he entered the Chapel partly in response to our talking about his persecution of Drake and my reproving him.

ROSS

You did WHAT?

DEMELZA

That is precisely what I did, no more than he deserved. He accepted it with a mixture of self-possession and humility. I too am surprised meeting a different person from the George I was accustomed to.

Ross

We are on a knife's edge, we all risk losing our poise.

Demelza

Can we trust George?

Ross

Can we trust ourselves? I have come to know George a great deal better: certain positive qualities in his nature, I think, were always there, hidden. Did you notice I now handle myself better than I used to?

Demelza

And I feel closer to Elizabeth, we need her to be confident, reliably firm but I find her wavering, confused.

Ross

You with Elizabeth and I with George are a strong side, if trust for one another holds. Destiny has thrown this dice: I would not have chosen to be so close to him, it is scary. When will you visit Morwenna?

Demelza

Tomorrow morning.

Ross

Please be careful to listen and be mindful of what you say to Elizabeth: we do not know what George has told her.

Demelza holds herself very close to Ross and lays her face on his chest, he caresses her auburn hair as if to protect and comfort her.

2i   Ext. Day
Ross and Demelza

Auburn hair emerging from the meadow: Ross and Demelza are strolling around checking the house and the stable, the sea is in the distance. They hold hands happily, as the zoom closes in we start to hear their conversation.

Ross

… Julia walking along the cliff path with me. She had a flowing dress, pale blue with dark blue ribbons. I saw her walking too close to the edge and moved to pick her up but she slid and fell. Before hitting the ground she began to fly her robe spreading like wings. It was a happy, colourful dream.

Demelza *excitedly*

How old was she?

Ross

Two, a little older than the age she died at AND the dream reminded me I had seen her just after she died. I was sitting with you at night, worrying you may die as well. I was exhausted, desperate (she pulls him closer and strokes him). There is no justice: you were kindly helping Francis family and their illness struck you as well. Julia died of it; I cursed life, God, everybody. Misery and death surrounded me, it was a wretched time and my enemies prospered. I had kept my life sober, my hands clean: what for? Anyhow, I remember I saw Julia (she had been dead a few hours) playing with the dog in the garden. I cannot explain it away: the dog was really playing with her.

(Ross sits down) Demelza *standing by him:*

I saw her too, briefly, in the kitchen once. I did not tell you as you were grieving for her.

Ross *continues*

There is more: she came towards me and she said clearly:

     He makes light and darkness,

      He grants joy and sorrow,

     He gives life and takes it away.

     I am in His garden now, I shall protect your lives.

I think she did too, when the Jury found me not guilty. How could I forget her blessing?

Demelza

Julia's life, her presence was more than joy, at times she seemed like a flash of light. Julia has been in this house all along, a tiny candle.

Ross

I fought, I cursed God, anger kept me alive. I fought through the night.

DEMELZA

In the morning God helped you and George reach an outcome that seemed impossible; he did not speak but he was there.

ROSS

George prayed at the end asking for His help, yes we both felt Him there. He responds to our call in the manner he chooses. He remained silent; I had been fighting with him: that is how it goes between us[50].

DEMELZA

He hopes we'll freely answer Him one day and he waits, he can wait longer than you can fight.

ROSS

He cannot force me to believe in Him, it wouldn't be fair.

DEMELZA

He could if he so wished.

With these words she scampers down the path and Ross runs after her; when he catches her they fall down together, laughing.

---

50   See the Bible's story of Jacob who fought all night long with "an angel".

ACT 3[51]

Human nature is abominable, even one's own (a statement by Ross)[52]

3a   Int. Nampara's library Day
Ross

The letter that follows is read by narrator with George's voice; Ross is pacing up and down the library. His commentary is spoken by him, but as the voice reads the letter he is silent, his face reacting to the content. (Images of the mine, of George watching Elizabeth with Ursula may interleaf).

Dear Ross no matter how difficult it is for me to write this letter I am certain it would prove impossible to say to you in person what I am about to write[53]. I did, as you suggested, obtain suitable clothing to go down the Weald Grace mine, now closed. I was accompanied by Hernshaw who warned me that it could be dangerous. It was desolate, dark and there was water everywhere. I talked to Hernshaw about the miners and learnt that half of them had found work with you but the other half starved, both the men and their families. I was told this was a mild winter and most survived, some have moved away. I employ a lot of people in the County and I am only able to do so because my business is profitable. I was a little grieved the consequences on the villagers were so severe; I had not taken time to consider them. As an investor I, too, take risks of heavy losses, even the debtor's prison. (Ross becomes irritable: *Is this supposed to mean he regrets the locals starving? Can't see him in a debtor's prison in a thousand years*). I remember you asking me not so long ago if I knew what the word guilt meant, ironically. I have of late felt some shame but little sense of responsibility. I could not help it: I had to close the mine, it had become unprofitable.

Walking around in the dark I started to shiver and felt a little afraid. For a mo-

---

51   All now mysterious shall be bright at last
       Be still my soul, the waves and wind still know
       His voice who ruled them while he dwelt below
       Second verse of the song Be still my soul sang to "Finland" Sibelius' tune

52   Graham W. 1977, *The Four Swans* (p.98), Ross is speaking to Dwight who is of the opinion that man always fails in his ideals due to Original Sin (sounds like Mother).

53   Camera pointing out of the window shows George in the distance trotting with Valentine in front of him on the saddle – we see them, Ross does not.

ment, I thought I saw a body floating on the water: it came towards me his face shimmering. It was Francis' face and then it vanished. I told my guide I wished to turn back.

I had not moved to ruin Francis financially for Elizabeth's sake, but he must have been dreading the power I had over him and escaped in the only way possible. This I believe holds true even if his death was accidental[54]. On the way home, I started to feel I was looking at myself and I was the bloated body in the water. One day I, shall be dead and only need the same small space in the cemetery as everyone else. I will no longer have my clothes, mines, servants and houses. A fool may inherit and mismanage them. Again I imagined myself as a corpse in the water. (Ross *This sounds more hopeful*). Suddenly my effort to impress and gain approval in good society seemed to me childish. All the clothes, the furnishings, the entertaining became cheap and squalid tricks anyone would see through. To obtain some advantages I had been flattering people I despise and lying to the few people I care for, working really hard for riches I could use to entice worthless associates, people who are for sale. I let myself be bought not by money but by prestige, recognition and the hope of being connected with powerful, respected people. I continued to feel alone and uncomfortable in good society. Not all the prizes I wanted could be bought with money.

Initially I felt shame as if, despite the attention to detail and the effort I had put into my clothing, standing in front of a tall mirror my appearance were utterly inappropriate. The shame was followed by a surge of guilt and I became angry with myself I felt I deserved retribution. I turned the anger from myself to external events or other people, working out how all this might be somebody else's fault. I know how easy it is to make a victim look at fault. When I arrived home I was in a dreadful mood. It caused everyone to hide from me but Elizabeth was so involved with rocking Ursula to sleep that she barely greeted me and did not notice the storm clouds in my eyes.

I would probably have vented my anger on the next person I spoke to, as I have often done in the past. I continued to watch them: admiration became reverence for this delicate and unbreakable bond "for love is as strong as death"[55]. The child fully trusting her mother; Elizabeth holding her with care paying attention to Ursula falling asleep as if nothing else mattered in this world. I doubt my mother ever held me with that intensity. I longed to be held as Ursula was, and comforted and forgiven. (Ross *Heavens, George is human after all!*) Believe me when I say that at that moment I felt held and loved by an invisible power.

---

54   An admission of moral responsibility for Francis' death is implied.

55   Well known quote from the biblical Song of Songs.

Something inside me stood still: "Where are those thine accusers? Hath no man condemned thee? – No man, Lord. – Neither do I condemn thee: go, and sin no more"[56]. I was not drunk, I did not hear a voice but it felt as if a voice had spoken, quietly and with authority: "Sin no more": so help me God.

Having lowered Ursula into the cot Elizabeth turned to me and saw I was moved. She lightly touched my arm; I lost control of my emotions and cried like a child with regret and with relief. I thought you would be glad to hear of this …miracle? Spiritual experience? I assure you it was real and it has changed me. I felt so much love embracing me, surrounding me like a stream of water. I never thought this may happen, not to me.

You may try it sometime, though it may not be to your liking. The guilt and the shame are still troubling me, but they now feel bearable and the wish to kill myself is not as strong. It was born of proud despair and of the fear I may be unable to change.

I do not mean to excuse myself for the damage I have done, for the injuries to Francis, to you and to my family. I accept there will be lasting consequences for all of us, outcomes of my past decisions and of my actions that cannot be undone.

Acceptance has taken the place of rage and despair. I have you to thank for helping me along this path. I will not regret it nor shall you.

Your humble servant George.

Ross

I have great difficulty imagining George as humble but he may be on his way there. I don't mind the road he takes or the sparks of lightening as long as we reach the right place. Looking out of the window Ross sees George trotting away at some distance from the house carrying Valentine, who appears happy and excited, on his horse. Ross paces the floor looking puzzled and a little concerned. He looks out of the window again, then goes outside towards the stable. George's horse has disappeared.

---

56 A quote from *John's gospel*, chapter 8: the learned Pharisees have sentenced a convicted adulteress to stoning, according to the Law. They ask Jesus: "Teacher, the Law says we should stone her, what do you say?" They think: got you, you damned hypocrite. If you say stone her where is your mercy? And if not are you condoning sin? (Jesus will in the same chapter later attack them as murderers, children of the Devil and tell them "You will die in your sin"). He replies: "He who is without sin may throw the first stone!" They all left the scene one by one and he said to the woman: "Woman has no one condemned you?" "No one, sir". "Then neither do I condemn you, go and leave your life of sin" (John 8, 3-11).

Narrator's *voice* (Ross) *speaking during the latter activity*

I shall return this letter personally, so it remains in his possession. Would I likewise trust him with my distress, my regrets? Am I looking at myself, the results of my actions which cannot be undone and the consequences for Elizabeth? His words have the ring of truth; I am flattered by his esteem. Am I willing to assist him? He assumes I am. Who can help me? Where is my inner voice, the guide George says took hold of him? He even jests that I would not like it. George writes of a shiver: fear and contrition. Such feelings must have been developing in his mind long before they overwhelmed him. God or the Devil may have given him a jolt or it could have been Francis' ghost's doing.

3b   Morwenna's tea Int. Day
Morwenna, Demelza and Elizabeth

Elizabeth and Demelza knock at Morwenna's door.
She welcomes them in a modest, tidy parlour tea and scones are on the table, a pleasant and relaxed meeting observed from outside the window. Camera enters the room as the conversation becomes more relevant: we can now hear them.

Elizabeth

Shall we break the ice and enter this delicate area? I know we encouraged you to marry Osborne. We assumed it would be a good situation for you and we gave you a dowry. It did not turn out as expected and we saw you were very unhappy.

Morwenna

Unhappy is too mild a word. For a time I (being naïve) thought rape was all there was in marriage. Yes that is how it started and continued, with his little prayers at the foot of the bed beforehand. His talk of marital duties made me feel guilty even suicidal. My stepdaughters were a comfort. When he got me with child I felt my body had been invaded and colonised. I felt another Osborne-monster growing his tentacles inside my belly.

Morwenna brought her hand to the lower abdomen and stared at the teapot. An attempt to sip her tea led to spilling it on the table.
Morwenna

There is fog before my eyes. When I suspected he was being unfaithful during the pregnancy, as he could not rape me, I was relieved. After the birth I felt dead inside dragging my body round the house. Do you know he tried to have me committed to a madhouse when I refused him his marital rights? I was in hell, with no one to turn to after Doctor Enys could not attend me any longer.

ELIZABETH *in some distress*
You could have turned to me.

MORWENNA
I thought you would lecture me about obedience to one's husband judging from the way you behave with George.

Elizabeth feels hurt by her comment and falls silent.

DEMELZA
Anyone would have helped if you had said then what you are saying to us now.

MORWENNA
I could not even find words I felt so ashamed. Every time he raped me I had a little less confidence, in the end I regarded myself as a broken doll fit only to be thrown away.

ELIZABETH *asked*
What of your books, of your education, were they of no help?

MORWENNA
He scorned them saying Greek was of no use to a woman who should take pride in her domestic skills.

DEMELZA *unable to control her anger*
What did George obtain in return for this despicable marriage?

ELIZABETH
Why do you blame my husband? We were only helping her.

MORWENNA *intervened*
George wanted to stop me from marrying below my class with Drake and by my marriage he obtained a connection to the Godolphins, on Osborne's maternal side. They are influential at Court.

DEMELZA, *turning to Elizabeth*
So you see he furthered his interest at the cost of Morwenna's sexual torture!

ELIZABETH *assertively*
You forget I was involved as well; we simply did not suspect Osborne was such a hypocrite.

MORWENNA

I believe you but I think George may have had an inkling, being a man, that something was amiss in his attitude to women. Osborne was as interested in women's feet as in their bodies,

I felt like a dead butterfly pinned in a collector's case; I was slowly dying. It took me many years, after he died and I married Drake to gradually recover some self-respect. I am glad I could be open with you. I see you sympathize with my experience and do not despise me. *She paused and covered her face with her hands.* Leaving my child with Osborne's mother was a relief though I feared she would spoil him in the same way as she twisted his father's mind.

ELIZABETH *in anger*

I cannot see how a woman may be willing to part from her small child. It is unnatural.

DEMELZA *blushing in anger*

I can see how often women are blackmailed and their attachments are misused to control their bodies and their minds.

MORWENNA

Our husbands are so different: all of them considerate towards us. I should count it as a blessing.

DEMELZA *apparently determined to quarrel with Elizabeth who pretends not to understand*

Without pretending everything is perfect when it is far from being so.

ELIZABETH

Morwenna I am sorry I was unwittingly responsible for your misfortune. Anything I can do to repair my mistake I'll do gladly. You are family and you will always be able to rely on us.

MORWENNA

I know. Demelza helped Carne and you have always assisted me. I hope I may some time be of service in return.

With this polite conclusion the encounter is successfully brought to a close but Elizabeth's leave taking from Demelza was cold.

3c   Int. Trenthwith sitting room Day
George and Elizabeth

Cut to Elizabeth and George sitting at ease, after dinner, by the fireplace.

ELIZABETH

There is something I'd like to know. Did you suspect Osborne would turn out to be such a dreadful man when we encouraged Morwenna to wed?

GEORGE

Why should I?

ELIZABETH

Because you are so perceptive of human weaknesses.

GEORGE

Because I have a vast experience of them?

ELIZABETH *does not smile at his jest but continues purposefully*

Morwenna told us in detail how Osborne abused her showing neither kindness nor respect for her mind and body. I felt we were somehow responsible for pressing her to take the decision to marry; she was so young. I was following your lead. Should I not have questioned your views?

GEORGE

That is what I loved you for: at first you were easily led and never questioned my decisions.

ELIZABETH

I feel a wife should support and praise her husband. Should she do so even if he is mistaken?

GEORGE *in mock horror:*

A frowning woman in my house in place of the husband-fearing wife I had a minute ago?

ELIZABETH

This is a serious matter, George.

GEORGE

Yes, the decision proved an error but was made in good faith.

ELIZABETH

Should I have listened to Morwenna's doubts and opposed you? Was this course followed to contrast Drake, Demelza's brother's, suit?

GEORGE

I was determined the marriage should take place; I gave her the dowry as you will recall.

ELIZABETH

What return did you get from that investment?

GEORGE's *attention drifts to her unspoken thoughts. Is her tone less than friendly?*
Why, we strengthened our, your family's connections.

ELIZABETH

With the Godolphins?

GEORGE

Yes he was right, Elizabeth is critical of him.
Anyway it is all past. I have told you how I apologised to Carne driven by an impulse I felt after Demelza spoke severely to me. He forgave me, as did Demelza. Please apologise to Morwenna on my behalf for our mistake. I'll be very pleased when this round of apologies is complete. *(Reflective pause).* Elizabeth I have considered my motives: I disliked the notion of Carne making friends with Geoffrey Charles and Morwenna because he was Demelza's brother and socially inferior. I should not have had him charged and imprisoned: the charge of theft was fabricated. I had to yield to Ross' threats and allow Drake to go free.
I may have pressed on with the marriage as a reprisal against Ross but I did not desire and I could not have anticipated that it would be such a disaster for Morwenna. I thought we were helping her gain a suitable husband. Yes we exerted much pressure on her. I would prefer that you apologise to her: a woman talking to a woman on a private and sensitive matter.

ELIZABETH *hesitating*

I decided to speak to you after Demelza made a sharp comment about your benefitting from Morwenna's unhappiness.

GEORGE

If you spoke to me sometimes, when appropriate, with severity it would help me assess my motives. I would rather it came from you than from anybody else.

ELIZABETH

I resented Demelza criticising you.

GEORGE

She is right, though. I have often used other people to my advantage without thinking of the consequences for them. A great deal of the damage thus caused is beyond repair.

ELIZABETH

For us this is in the past but Morwenna will carry the scars of her wounds.

GEORGE

Nothing we can do will change this.

ELIZABETH

Should we not seek a change that can be made?

GEORGE

Please explain this to me.

ELIZABETH

I should like to avoid a similarly distressing experience for a young, unprotected woman. You know they have a workhouse in Bodmin. There is a prejudice against girls who have spent their childhood there. As a consequence they cannot enter into service and be guided, they often run wild. I suggest you find a way of having suitable girls apprenticed to tradespeople, say to a seamstress, making it clear they are under our protection and if they be in any way molested we would show our displeasure. I, for my part, may employ one or two of those same girls in my house as servants taking care of their moral and domestic instruction personally.

GEORGE

The objection people have is that these girls are tainted by the sin of their mothers.

ELIZABETH

If you can think of a better way to make amends for the mistake we made I'll be glad to follow it but you may allow me to decide on this occasion; as for people's malice targeting innocent girls I am certain we should have no part in it.

GEORGE

My wife directing some penance for our sins, what a shameless piece of insubordination! *At this she finally smiled, knowing he was in a happy mood and in agreement with her.* Even your criticism is gentle.

ELIZABETH

George, I forgot: a letter came for you today, it is on the sideboard as It was not taken to your desk.

She stands up and takes the letter to him, he opens it unhurriedly.

GEORGE

Just a note from Francis Basset wishing to discuss some business at his bank tomorrow; my affairs must not spoil our evening.

Cut to Elisabeth brushing her hair in her bedroom and George entering dressed in a bright Indian cloth dressing gown. Beginning of a love scene.

3d   Int. New Cornish bank Day
Harris, Ross, Francis Basset, George

The camera follows Ross (in Truro's streets) going to his friend's home via a bustling market place.

NARRATOR

Cary Warleggan had all but put Pascoe's bank out of business before Ross had intervened and convinced (with a determination which surprised Demelza) Francis Basset, Baron de Dunstainville, to put into effect a fusion between his Bank and Pascoe's. Harris' position was preserved but he lost his money due to the run on his bank carefully prepared and fuelled by Warleggan bank. Uncle Cary did the dirty work. George had felt uneasy but could deny any involvement: he had been away at the time.

Francis Basset disliked Warleggan's sharp, unprincipled practices. George judged Francis to be a little old fashioned and Pascoe even worse, unable to move with the times. Due to Francis Basset's reconciliation with Lord Falmouth George had had lost the election in Truro two years earlier and Ross had become Truro's MP. As a consequence George had to go to considerable expenses to set himself up in another seat. His bank had financed his ambitions despite Uncle Cary's protests that the expenditure led to temporary cash flow difficulties for their bank (a closely guarded secret).

3d This scene interleaves a conversation Ross-Harris Pascoe at Pascoe's home with the conversation George-Francis Basset at the bank, the former friendly the latter stormy

The Ross-Harris conversation at Pascoe's home is required in order to explain the background; a little later they will turn up at the bank and intervene.

NARRATOR

Ross had been looking forward to seeing his old friend happy again after the collapse of Pascoe's bank had been somehow remedied with a fusion under Basset's auspices and Pascoe had become a partner in the new Cornish bank.

Camera: an elderly female servant opens the door and introduces Ross into Harris's studio.

HARRIS

Welcome Ross! I was about to go to work at my new bank. I still have not properly thanked you for convincing Francis Basset's bank to agree a fusion between his bank and mine. *Angrily he went on* It is now clear to me how Cary engineered a run on my funds: as you recall my daughter Joan's husband had a considerable amount of money deposited in my bank. Cary Warleggan lent him a large sum and withdrew it suddenly; I had to give him back his deposit to cover the loan. He moved just after notary Pearce died and it was discovered that he had embezzled some of the money held on trust in my bank. He was such an old friend I did not think to check his work closely; his mind was clouded by the illness. Anonymous letters arrived to my customers questioning my professional competence and the soundness of Pascoe's bank. People started withdrawing money and I could not find anyone to help, except for your wife.

ROSS

I came home from London and believed the battle lost. Do you think Warleggan bank may have had inside information on your affairs?

PASCOE

That I do not know but they pulled out all the stops, as they had done once before, in order to destroy the bank's financial standing and my reputation partly, I presume, because of our fast friendship.

ROSS

I do not give up easily and Basset was dismayed when I told him how your ruin was engineered.

Initial phase of Basset's and George's conversation here (cut to 3d A)

HARRIS

What truth is there in the rumours of reconciliation between Trentwith and Nampara, of conversation between you and George?

ROSS

It is all true, we are reconciled. I climbed down first and George followed.

HARRIS

How astonishing. Are you pleased?

ROSS

Very, and so is Demelza. We may get an invitation to little Ursula's Christening! I was intending to return a document George has given me which he needs.

HARRIS

You may meet him at the Cornish bank (in truth Basset's bank) this morning; He has arranged a meeting with Francis. Let's walk, it is close.

Cut to 3d B

3d A

George walking swiftly enters the Cornish bank, expecting a business inquiry. Francis stiffly shows him into his office.

GEORGE *pleasantly*

I see you have a very comfortable office here.

FRANCIS, *icily*

Yes, with new partners. We did lose a clerk whom I believe you now employ. *(George thinks Francis does not know that this clerk had been Cary's spy in Pascoe's bank, but he is wrong).*

FRANCIS

I'll come straight to the point. You must know how Pascoe's bank was the butt of your financial offensive. I have no doubt you were also behind the anonymous letters which started a run on the bank. A questionable and distasteful strategy, ungentlemanly. I recall it all happened once before, during the crisis of the bank of England. When I think the country is fighting for its liberty I am shocked so much energy and venom has been put into this private settling of scores. You will guess from the fact that Pascoe and Poldark are listed as partners in this Bank that I am on their side.

GEORGE

This is an appalling misunderstanding! In fairness you should give me a chance to reply to serious allegations. I was not in Truro at the time.

FRANCIS

I cannot see any possible defence. I have been making inquiries all summer and so have others. Your considerable ability to dissemble and mislead will only embitter me further. You may be a rising star but I am one of the most influential people in this county.

GEORGE

No one disputes that. I perceive it was not business you wished to talk about today.

FRANCIS

On the contrary. This is the very foundation of business: the frames governing decent men's interaction in politics and commerce, without which we are no better than highwaymen; they too inspire awe and amass wealth till the day they hang.

Here: second and last segment of Ross and Pascoe's conversation – they walk to the bank

3d B

FRANCIS

Incidentally your practices did not endear you to some gentlemen. That's why you lost the parliamentary election to Lord Falmouth's candidate Ross Poldark.

GEORGE *clearly annoyed*

That may be better explained by the fact that my family tree does not go back to the Norman Conquest.

FRANCIS

Permit me to say that you are quite wrong: a number of traders whose business has prospered only recently are respected for their reputable conduct and values: the Warleggans are feared. I may have started to fear them myself after I saw what they are capable of.

GEORGE
It grieves me you doubt my loyalty and sincere respect.
George now sees that Francis is really annoyed
I wish to dispel the clouds hanging over our friendship.

FRANCIS
As I do not!

(George was a little relieved to see – through the glass of the door – Harris Pascoe and Ross appear in the next room).

FRANCIS *sarcastically*
I think it is appropriate to invite our friends into the room.

GEORGE
I would be glad of it.

FRANCIS
I did not know you were friendly with either of them!

GEORGE
Communication between Trentwith and Nampara has greatly improved.

After a brief round of salutations they are sitting around a mahogany table which Francis thumps with his hands, angrily.

GEORGE *(to Harris and Ross)*
I am sorry to say I have displeased Francis chiefly on account of the collapse of Pascoe's bank.

HARRIS
Which Warleggan bank brought about!

Before George has time to protest Francis adds:
FRANCIS
What you do not understand is that your role as a notable and affluent family should not merely be attending to your business. Trade depends on the security and prosperity of the common people and a frame of shared aims and values. You are not concerned with either. The spreading of your influence supports practices close to blackmail which I cannot condone. Your only purpose is expanding and maximizing profits. Associates and clients are regarded as nothing

more than puppets. You should also be concerned with the general progress and comfort of ordinary people. Being secretly cursed by them carries a risk, even a commercial risk.

GEORGE

Francis we could both end up saying things we may later regret. It would be sensible to continue the conversation at a time when you are better disposed towards the Warleggans.

There is a short, tense silence. Francis calls for drinks to be brought but he is not appeased:

FRANCIS

Unless I am satisfied that your sharp practices will cease I intend to move against your interests. I know you are in a weaker financial position having spent money to support your return to Parliament.

GEORGE

I did nothing improper.

FRANCIS

You acquired properties in a parliamentary Borough in order to be elected as an MP. Some may find it improper, even illegal but it is a path often trodden. Let us suppose someone sends some anonymous letters to your clients suggesting you may not be solvent any more…

Ross

Francis I am mystified. Has anything happened I am not aware of? Why are you so annoyed with George?

FRANCIS

Do not tell me you wish to defend him or you Harris, do you intend to side with George? If I say we can move on Warleggan bank due to their weakness I know what I am doing.

Ross

Why would you do this? It involves risk and will cause a great deal of conflict in the county; can't we compose what differences you are having? I believe George is open to a compromise.

GEORGE

I am willing to meet Francis half way but he seems very annoyed with me and

I feel I don't deserve these threats. Has my bank profited from the closure of Pascoe's Bank? I don't think so.

(Ross sees George's shield being raised and the risk of his retreating behind defensive walls; is Basset's threat a sally or a declaration of war?)

ROSS

Francis what is the aim of this conversation?

FRANCIS

To stop the Warleggans even thinking of doing to us what they did to Harris: destroying the reputation of a good man who had served the county honestly for thirty years. Nobody will stand up to them anymore: there is only myself and Lord Falmouth left in the field.

GEORGE

And Captain Poldark... Commerce and banking are in many ways akin to war: there are winners and losers. My family's fortune has grown by taking opportunities and paths which had not been taken before, we also took risks and we might have failed.

FRANCIS

By new paths you mean the use of slanderous anonymous libels?

GEORGE

The slander comes from you, there is no proof those letters were from us.

FRANCIS

Many will think so, do you deny it?

GEORGE

I did not come to hear my family business put in the dock. I can respond for my actions as a respected banker and trader. If you call me to account then you offer evidence. If I have made mistakes I can accept correction but I shall not swallow insults.

FRANCIS

By calling in debts owed to you Warleggan bank made Pascoe's position untenable. No bank can return all the money to investors in a short time, your own bank included, as you may soon find out.

Ross *to Harris (trying to shift the conversation and avoid a fight)*

I have been damaged by the closure of Pascoe's bank too and I have tried to remedy this as best I could: we managed this fusion thanks to the goodwill of Francis Basset and other gentlemen who continue to esteem you, Harris.

Harris *(almost ignoring the other two, turning to Ross, his tone of voice angry)*

And dislike the Warleggans for breathing down traders' necks; their motivation for causing my heavy losses owes little to commercial competition and a lot to personal animosity. I have come by much confidential information in my long life and supported you, Ross, and your father before you.

Ross *sternly*

Harris, I have spent my time and my reputation helping your cause and I may agree with your sentiments. I do not think a rift arising between two of the most influential men in this town can be in anybody's interest. I nearly quarrelled with George over their ambush to your former bank recently but we have since mended our rift at a personal level. I think questions need to be asked about Warleggan bank's intrigues. The people who can answer these questions are Nicolas, George and Cary.

Francis

It would be hard for me to believe their answers. I have evidence of George's duplicity.

George

Francis, the truth cannot always be told particularly in business.

Francis

True but I find your opinion chiefly self-serving, you have a manifest ability to deceive and flatter.

George

Many wish to be flattered, others deceive themselves. If you will take my word...

Francis abruptly interrupts him:

Francis

Your word does not count for very much in this room. *George winces visibly.*

George

A regrettable state of affairs which I have recently decided to remedy. How can I make you believe my words and my desire to be on good terms with all of you?

Ross guesses that Francis' offensive is so hurtful that George is on the verge of running away.

Ross

Your wish to reach an understanding does you credit: I believe you George. Francis does not, do you Harris?

Harris

If you say you believe George I'll go along with you.

Francis *with stern authority*

Gentlemen I am stunned by your moderation. As you are the injured party I will take notice of your restraint. I can give George the benefit of the doubt this one last time if, speaking on behalf of his father and his uncle, he now undertakes not to repeat behaviour such as throwing somebody's promissory notes on the market, asking suddenly for debts to be covered as a form of pressure, cutting off normal credit co-operation, ceasing to discount bills without good reason and using anonymous libels. I need it in writing with three Warleggan signatures. Remember you cannot blame Cary if something goes wrong, I'll hold you responsible for what your Bank and your agents do. You'll have to control your uncle somehow.

In your other business operations you George personally undertake not to use unjustified financial pressure or blackmail of any kind.

George

I do not use blackmail prove your charge! You have no evidence.

George's self-restraint is waning.

Harris

If you wish me to provide the evidence I am happy to meet in private or with you and Ross but I cannot disclose my source of information. It is possible, but unlikely, you may not be fully informed of your uncle's initiatives.

Francis *politely but angrily*

Some form of apology to Mr Pascoe at the next meeting of the Cornish bank would be greatly appreciated, if any of you can bring himself to attend. I suggest your father might wish to: if these agreements are kept we shall not move against your bank. If I see any of them broken I will aim to cause as much damage as I can to your interest, keeping within legal bounds of course.

George

You have stated your requests and I shall do my best to obtain my relative's agreement and signatures. Ross I am obliged to you for the trust and support you gave me just now.

Ross moves closer and speaks to George confidentially, as if they were having a private conversation.

ROSS

It was my intention to return a document I received from you recently. I think it is better if you keep it: you may wish to destroy it. *He hands the letter he received back to George.* I have read this carefully, I do not express myself well in writing but I'll try to reply. I am glad to have your trust.

FRANCIS *more relaxed, addressing George coldly*

I am happy to see the understanding and support Ross has offered you, George. I am pleasantly surprised by your co-operation and openness. How long will it be before you return with the draft of the statement I suggested?

GEORGE

Within 48 hours I hope. Both Ross and myself have changed Francis I am glad you have noticed it.

FRANCIS *stiffly*

I have an engagement, I'll leave you to make your arrangements.

As Francis Basset goes out of the bank the camera follows him.

HARRIS O/S

I also need to attend to business in my office. You'll find me there.

Ross and George are left in the office.

GEORGE O/S

Let's go elsewhere! *George is seen walking out.*

Ross *(following George) ironical:*

Do you not like our new Cornish bank?

Ross follows him to a private room in a nearby inn, they sit comfortably.

GEORGE

I am glad I got out of there alive, largely thanks to you.

Ross *interrupts him*

Largely thanks to your negotiating skills and your patience; the dividends of a little honesty, George.

GEORGE

You believed me and urged others to believe my words when Francis insulted me.

Ross

I have believed you for some time now and you honoured me with your trust and this letter. I'd prefer you to meet Pascoe on your own. He is a kind man. You were able to handle Francis; I imagine you can reach an understanding with Harris. Mind, he'll not forgive you for bankrupting him, not yet, you need to work for it and not let us down. Remember we are all still a little afraid of you, even Francis!

GEORGE

A **little**? You ought to be very frightened of George. Now that am seeing him in daylight he scares me too! And I need to live with him!
George was dazed, unsmiling. Ross detected a shiver.
Will you not come with me when I talk to Pascoe?

As he gives his reply Ross moves to face him and holds him close, his hand on George's wide shoulder, his tone is challenging:

Ross

I supported you against Francis; I did not know he planned to move on your bank and I am glad we may have avoided it. As to what the Warleggans did to Harris Pascoe and his bank you avoided giving answers just now but I have spent the summer months trying to help my good friend and I have a fair knowledge of what may have happened. I am still very angry about it and I am certain that if I came in with you I would lose my temper. I recall saying last summer within your hearing and despite Dwight signalling to me to stay calm that corrupt power had been corruptly employed. You replied that Harris Pascoe was a silly old man who had no business to have charge of large sums of money when we were sitting at the table, at the opening of the Infirmary. Only Elizabeth's fainting prevented a blazing row on that occasion. *(The memory brings back the anger he had felt)*. Now count yourself lucky that this "silly old man", a lifelong friend of mine, is also a very good man. I cannot be present at your meeting: I am barely in control of myself now. In truth, were I not beholden to you and Elizabeth, my desire would be to stay as far away from you as I can.

George looks stunned and Ross knows he must restore their bond:

Ross *drawing George closer*
> We must hold on to one another and maintain trust; else all we have gained is lost.

Once more George buried his face on Ross' shoulder for perhaps one minute, then, looking away, he spoke slowly, in the fashion he might have chosen in the past until his unease grew and anger with himself surfaced.
GEORGE
> I have more money, ability, social influence than you both. My business is vastly more successful than Pascoe's who has been leading a prudent and predictable life. We have been innovative; he was often a critic and an obstacle. He saved you financially when you were opposing us. It was natural for me to try to cut him down to size, attack his reputation, ruin him and enjoy his defeat and humiliation, enjoy seeing him lower his head. You explained to me why this is wrong. I am starting to agree with your views but I continue to enjoy my dominance and despise a defeated rival.

Ross *conciliatory*
> You are ahead of me now. Your esteem for me, your trust and affection taking me into your private world, gazing at your conceit and passing judgement on your attitude makes me feel that you are like a brother to me, like an older brother who has achieved what I am aiming for: to look at myself with a sober and compassionate insight. The next step for you is look at a mirror others are offering you, where your image is reflected in unexpected shapes and consider the marks you have left on your victims.

GEORGE *bitterly*
> I am sick and tired of being humiliated first by Basset, then by you and later by Pascoe. Your generosity humbles me: I wish to crawl away and hide.

Ross *replied with a tranquil, firm tone*
> Listen now, George, I am not going to make allowance for false pride. Harris and, indirectly, I were the people you wished and managed to hurt. We have just now helped you to stall an attack from Francis. There is no need for you to speak to Harris, it was his suggestion and you may not take it up at all or just wait till you feel ready to do so.

GEORGE *quietly*
> I am as ready as I shall ever be. You clearly think I should.

Ross
You decide.

George *stood up, holding the back of the chair and looking at his shoes*
No! You decide. I can yield if you answer kindly.

Ross
Harris would like to put his case and you to listen. He is not asking you to agree with him or apologize. I think he deserves your attention and he is entitled to some answers.

George *standing, more relaxed*
Your anger just now has reminded me that this tension is hard for you to face, as testing as it is for me. I'll steel myself to talk to Harris. I'll answer him. Please remember I am only facing this trial because I seek your trust and your esteem.

Ross *deeply moved shakes his hand:*
You already have those. Patience and candour will be more useful to you than steel.

George *visibly upset touched his arm and took his leave quickly:*
I bid you good day.

Ross
Take good care of yourself.
Ross stayed and called the innkeeper ordering lunch, relieved he had been able to show his annoyance without hostility.
How much resentment from the past still needs to be laid to rest?
Ross asked himself aloud.

3e   Int. The Warleggans' bank Day
George and Nicolas[57]

George is sitting in his stately armchair and Nicholas is pacing slowly around the room, as if buried in thoughts.

GEORGE, *after heaving a sigh*

Father, do you recall the conversation we had by the cliffs on the subject of my soul's dark caves?

NICHOLAS

I was glad you took me in your confidence, I did not wish to intrude upon your inner thoughts.

GEORGE

Do not imagine that what I am about to say is a criticism of yourself. I have lately not followed your advice, which is my fault entirely. Achieving success, being respected and feared was my wish, I tolerated no obstacle. I followed a deliberate and hidden strategy seducing, bribing or slandering. Very few dared resist, if they did they were silenced. As my arrogance increased so did my disregard for truth, honesty, kindness and fairness. I have sinned both in my private life and in the conduct of business. I did not break the law or falsify the books but I did not follow your example of honourable business practice. I am sorry this implicates our Bank and you as well. Basset has rescued Pascoe, Ross Poldark has supported his old friend and we are blamed (rightly) for the scheming leading to Pascoe's bankruptcy. Basset, who virtually owns the Cornish bank, was determined to move against us. Ross and I have barely managed to stay his hand on certain conditions. Francis is a mild-mannered gentleman; I never saw him in such a fury before. He said he is frightened of us.

NICHOLAS

How on earth has Ross Poldark come to be on your side?

GEORGE

We have reconciled: after my wife nearly died I felt I had to examine myself, the inner spaces I called "my caves". I found the exploration frightening yet

---

57   "If I say 'surely the darkness will hide me and the light become night around me'
Even the darkness will not be dark to you
The night will shine like the day
For darkness is as light to you" Psalm 139 11-12

exciting, with pools of light within the darkness. I discovered those caves were an important part of my soul I could not cut out without being impoverished. I am learning to own my darkness, there are riches there too. Sins, mistakes are, I know, part of my fabric. I am ashamed to acknowledge this and I am now the critic of the person I have been. Ross has acknowledged his faults as well and in this process of self-understanding we have helped one another with kindly sincerity, patience and severity. I renounced the jealousy and desire for revenge I had long nurtured in my heart against him, as did he.

NICHOLAS *worried and probably not listening:*
Are Basset's terms negotiable?

GEORGE
I fear they are not; we shall have to limit uncle Cary's freedom of action as he is likely to stray. I have tried to hide behind him but I know my responsibilities. Pascoe has been very well informed by his spies. My private meeting with him was truly embarrassing; I had to concede: his allegations I knew to be true. I am becoming accustomed to being, as Basset said, cooperative. In legal terms I now hand myself in. This is what I am about to do with you, father. It will be the easiest and happiest confession I have ever offered knowing how fond and proud of me you are. It will not be, it never is, a full admission. I am only sad that it may cause you to be ashamed of your son.

NICHOLAS
No George, like the father of the prodigal son I can only rejoice and celebrate.

GEORGE
Father you seem afraid, unwilling to listen. You are the only person I can open my heart to. I need your advice, your affection, I need you to listen to my confession.

Nicholas is sitting comfortably in the armchair, by George's side, close but not looking at him. George is looking towards the window, blushing slightly, his initial courage spent.

GEORGE
As a young man I learned to control my tongue and my resentment hiding cold enmity with affable civility and striking hard when the occasion presented itself. My fortune and influence made me the object of admiration; making myself agreeable I seduced, enchanted. I was spoiled by praise to which I added silent self-worship. The flattery of the world, the arrogance of youth and the awareness of my success conspired to make me feel invincible. I had become my own idol,

careful not to display my power but wielding it without self-discipline. This magic was dissolved when I was not elected as Member of Parliament despite fully using our influence; Ross being elected added insult to injury. It showed me the limits of my strength. Being defeated did not lessen my conceit and increased my desire to take revenge on Ross. I undertook actions I can only regret now. Our feeling towards one another was truly close to murder. I pride myself on being mature and sensible but, had I not been thrashed, I was close to losing my common sense even my balance. I was still running away from my guilt when God came to me and offered his forgiveness demanding I renounce my self-worship, show sincere regret for my sins and keep faith with my repentance not by my strength, the little I have, by God's strength to whom I have surrendered.

George felt relief, paused and looked to his father who was fighting with tears.
GEORGE

Over the last few days I have accepted that I was an obstinate bastard and admitted how disgraceful some of my schemes have been. Today, receiving a few well-deserved lashes from three people, Ross one of them, I was indignantly refusing to take my bitter medicine. I am tired of humbling confessions; I must now alter both my attitudes and my actions. I need to change my resentment at being disciplined; acknowledge I was not struck as hard as I should have been. Ross had the audacity to say that he and Harris, whom I intended to hurt, helped me, stood by my side today and it was true... Why am I unable to tell, or show them I am grateful? It is my false pride and, yes, it must change.

With Ross so far we stood together and fought our fears, our anger. I see how tired and tense Ross is now, how close to losing control. I care for him as he cared for me. I cannot at this point ask him to bear my sorrow. I may well need to support him instead.

NICHOLAS

I know your stubbornness; it prevented you from listening to my words of advice. God knows I wished to spare you this bitter medicine you have had to swallow. I have paid close attention to what you've told me but I need to understand it before I can help you find a new path, with a changed heart. Now you are going to listen to me and your natural stubbornness can help you improve your conduct, your steady strength may serve a good purpose. Let us enjoy good wine and our new confidence and closeness. Later we can have an honest and stern conversation but now let me welcome you back George. I feared I had lost touch with you, I have found you again: a better man and a cherished son.

Nicholas touches his arm and George takes his hand, affectionately holding it, able to look his father in the eyes; both men are fighting back tears of joy.

There may be frames here indicating that Nicola and George continue to talk but we are not aware of what is being said, we can imagine it. The camera may see them through a pane of glass so the words are not heard.

3f Int. domestic scene in Nampara's breakfast room
Ross and Demelza
then Ext. (beach) Day
Ross, George and Valentine

Ross takes Elizabeth's letter and goes out, walking towards the cove reading it. Demelza is busy with the children. Dwight will be present when Ross returns: he has been called to check on Jeremy.
Going towards the beach Ross' pace is brisk, compatibly with reading and walking, his face increasingly showing annoyance and sorrow. Finally he sits on a rock by the edge of the sea. Behind him George on horseback (still in the distance) is trotting towards the shore with Valentine in front of him on the saddle.

NARRATOR'S *voice is* ELIZABETH'S

Dear Ross, I need to thank you for the support you are giving George. It has made a great difference to our lives. After the talk I had with Morwenna together with Demelza I have concluded that I need to forgive you partly for the sake of the friendship and the help you gave me in the past partly for the Christian duty of renouncing revenge and bitterness towards those who have offended us, as we pray every day in "Our Father".

The disclosure of Morwenna's sexual humiliation and her feeling soiled and injured by Oswald's abuse of his marital rights reminded me how frequently women less fortunate than myself have suffered such ill treatment; compared to theirs my misfortune was relatively benign. I considered whether I should have defended myself more forcefully but I concluded it might have led to more hurtful treatment on your part. I knew your temper could dominate you. The affection I still had for you at the time made it easier for you to break down my refusal and may have given you the impression that, after the initial assault, you were not injuring me. A mixture of fear and natural physical response to your advances did not signal agreement but made me feel cheap and humiliated. I experienced you taking possession of my entire person, body and mind. Then the worst happened and I knew I was pregnant before my marriage. I had no choice and much heartache. Learning to love my child was a struggle after he was born. Shaming you is not my purpose with such personal confidences, I would like you to understand my former reluctance and resistance to forgive just as I determine to put the past behind us for the sake of my family, of my soul and of my peace of mind.

I hope you will be able to accept my forgiveness in the same spirit of reconciliation in which it is offered. In return I wish you to discuss oftentimes with a wise friend the difficulties you have always had to be patient and hold your temper, hoping the prudence of maturity may also change you. I was reading an oriental novel and found a few lines which I think are relevant[58]: "He who feels overwhelmed by anger must reflect on what a wise man once said to a Sultan who had asked him for advice on how to control anger: it is necessary to remember one must obey as well as being obeyed, one must serve as well as being served, one must endure as well as being endured. Above all remember God always sees you".

God was the only one who saw us, He decided it should not be hidden; this has led to a positive outcome no one would have dared to hope for. God bless you Elizabeth[59].

Ross' immediate reaction was to feel vulnerable, rebuked and mutinous
NARRATOR – ROSS' *voice*

This is a bitter letter to swallow; it is hard mercy she offers. I do not wish to accept it. I feel angry. God is not at home nor do I wish to find out what his opinion is. What was he thinking of when he created humans, man and woman? Human nature is abominable. My temper is part of my personality and I was sorely provoked…

NARRATOR *ends*

Ross turns hearing a noise. He sees George approaching and helps him by lifting Valentine down from the horse,

---

58 Al-Gazali A. H. 2005, *La bilancia dell'azione* written in arabic around 1000 AD. "Chi si sente assalire dalla collera rifletta su quel che un saggio disse una volta a un sultano che gli aveva domandato, appunto, come difendersi dall'ira. É indispensabile rammentarsi che si deve anche ubbidire oltre che essere ubbidito e sopportare oltre che essere sopportato. Ricorda soprattutto che Dio sempre ti vede". English translation from the above Italian text is mine.

59 A part of her disbelieves the fact that Valentine is with certainty Ross' child. When she meets with George (whom she has asked to delay the marriage) on the 20th of May – the marriage takes place on June 20th – she must know it is possible she may be with child. She is perhaps waiting for Ross to visit again in order to tell him but this is not going to happen. She is, as a consequence of being pregnant, forced to marry someone, for the sake of the unborn child. This is alluded to by her statement (in the original novel) that she feels in a cage. Both men have put her in that cage, together. A possible defensive move by Elizabeth is to consider the child purely as her own child, her main attachment. The original text suggests that with her marriage to George "she is lost forever". Her tragedy remains hidden.

Ross

Out for a ride with father, Valentine?

VALENTINE

Uncle Ross I want to look at crabs in the rock pools.

Ross lowers him to the ground carefully and he runs off.

GEORGE

I thank you again for your help at the Cornish bank. Without you I might have sunk under Basset's fire. Now Cary is consigned to the dungeon and father will offer an apology to Pascoe. I reported what Francis Basset said. They understood the dangers of the Cornish Bank moving against us and agreed to sign. They could barely believe you shielded me. Father was understanding ever indulgent with me.

Ross

Your family agreed to sign and behave? It will not happen again?

GEORGE

It shall not. Have you been keeping well?

Ross confided:

I have read Elizabeth's letter: she is willing to forgive me but I am finding very hard to accept what she says.

GEORGE

This is between you and her, I find it impossible to comment. I try not to think about the past. You cannot accept what you see in the mirror Elizabeth is holding in front of you. I had the same problem with Pascoe and you steered me towards facing him when I was tempted to run away. You honoured me by calling me brother, if that was how you felt may I now speak freely?

Ross

We made a pact to speak the truth: if you mean to help me I am willing to listen. I must break this standstill.

GEORGE

You must accept her forgiveness. If you open your heart to it you should feel grateful. Truth cannot be avoided forever.

Ross
  This is precisely what I feel unable to do. I cannot, George.

George
  This translates as: I do not wish to. What is your next excuse?

Ross *despondently shrugging his shoulders:*
  This debate is useless.

Valentine comes running back holding some bark with small crabs on it.
Valentine
  Papa, look!

On hearing "papa" Ross feels as if somebody had punched him in the chest.

George *inspecting the crabs*
  This one is dead, I think. *Turning to Ross he adds with mock severity:*
  You stay on the beach and have a heart-to-heart with your good self. Remain
  here till you concede, else there will be no supper for you.

Valentine thinks his father is talking strangely to uncle who is clearly unhappy.
Valentine
  Can I stay on the beach with uncle Ross please? I don't want supper.

George
  That's up to uncle Ross. He can bring you home. *George turns to Ross:* Valentine
  will help your make up your mind.

Ross is speechless: obliged to remain on the beach with a child to mind, **the** *child?
George goes to untie his horse; he is already some distance away when Ross recovers his
ability to speak.*

Ross
  You can't be serious.

George
  Too late, he will prove a great help in your considerations. Ross you know what
  you must do. I sometime wonder how they made you obey orders in the army!

Ross
  Point taken.

George canters off and Valentine tries to interest Ross in the crab hunting.

NARRATOR

Ross follows Valentine on his trail of rock pools and discoveries of aquatic life, Valentine's chatter and memories of his own childhood mixing he feels relief, then quiet enjoyment. With Valentine climbing some rocks and running ahead he has time to re-read the letter, finding it less devastating than the first time he read *it. (Fragments of the letter are read aloud, he is mulling over them).*

NARRATOR *stops*

VALENTINE

Look here, this is part of a sail and a rope; it must be from a ship that went down in the gale. Do you remember?

ROSS

Yes, we had to repair the stable roof; I thought it lucky there was little damage to the house.

VALENTINE

Did you see the big waves? Have you ever seen bigger ones? I made a drawing of the storm at sea.

ROSS

Will you show it to me sometime?

He warms to the child, starts to forget the letter and engages in exploration. Later he takes Valentine back to Trentwith on horseback, giving him a letter he has quickly penned for Elizabeth[60].
He liked the closeness with the child sitting on his saddle. He knows in his heart an acceptance of the message conveyed in her letter has occurred, somehow.

3 g   Int. Nampara sitting room Day
Ross, Demelza, Dwight

ROSS

You never spoke of your conversation with Morwenna.

---

60   This is shown by a camera positioned at some distance from the scene, perhaps with fog coming from the sea. It is a childhood dreamland, akin to a lakes' district landscape in mist.

DEMELZA

It was so distressing; I thought Elizabeth was going to cry. Morwenna is brave; we helped her put her past suffering into words. What was in Elizabeth's letter?

ROSS

She forgave. She asked me to find one wise friend who'd help me reform. I thought Dwight very suitable.

DEMELZA *jokes*

I should not wish to have such a responsibility myself.

DWIGHT *also joking*

I shall need some inducement to undertake this hard and challenging task!

ROSS

I wish someone would take me seriously. (to Dwight) You'll remember our conversation when we met at the big oak. Let us take it from there. I am clearer about the problem now: I had to accept her point of view and reform mine to be able to accept her forgiveness.

DWIGHT

Do you have a time in mind for our meeting?

ROSS

A time and a subject matter: how does one forgive oneself?

DWIGHT

This topic I covered carefully, long ago[61].

I blamed myself for Karen's murder: I should have seen her husband would take revenge. I could not decide how much the fault for the seduction fell on me. When your baby daughter died, even more so when my eldest died I also blamed myself; rationally, as a doctor, I could see I had done everything possible but that did not take the tragedy away. We were warned at medical school that we should not put ourselves in God's place. We aim to step in his shoes and feel triumphant when we do succeed. One day we may come very close to His knowledge.

---

61   Dwight refers to an event in the *Demelza Poldark* novel: he was seduced by the wife of a miner who discovered it and in anger accidentally murdered her. The husband had to flee to save his life. Dwight felt responsible for her death.

Ross

A great danger for us: our selfish predatory nature barely held in check and our power immense. How did you heal and recover peace of mind?

Dwight

I stepped into God's shoes, dismissing the guilt and the whispers of my soul: I imagined the compassion and the forgiveness coming from Him, His healing power surrounding me. As a man lies in the sun and enjoys it I let him look at me and I tried to look back at him.

Ross

What does he look like then? Can you stare at the sun?

Dwight

I could not tell you. You will think me deluded or naïve but I felt the warmth and the forgiveness.

Ross *sarcastically*

Another one! This is an epidemic.

Dwight

Pardon?

Ross

Nothing, I was talking to myself. I believe this gentleman, God, has taken a dislike to me, he will not pay me a call. I find him irrationally hostile we were never in accord. I do not see him in the sun or anywhere else. The sea reminds me of infinity, of death; it comes close to eternity.

Demelza

Ross, we were talking of Julia, how she still lives in our home and cares for us, but we cannot see her. She is like an angel, a messenger. God may have reasons not to show himself to us.

Ross

Dearest we shall all die and if I should find anyone beyond that portal I'll ask "it" if I can come back and tell you! As for Julia she is now on his side, not on mine. Dwight my only possibility is learning to forgive myself. We must have a serious talk with my conscience, it must relent. We'll have negotiations and establish a peace treaty: we shall both be more agreeable.

I like the idea of both you and Demelza helping me, you have always tried to

96

but I could not accept it. Yes, with both of you it may work, my conscience may sue for peace.

DEMELZA

And you are willing to listen?

ROSS

I shall have to, according to Elizabeth.

DEMELZA

And according to me!

She looks out of the window having heard a cracking sound, she sees a large tree branch (which was broken by the wind) flying past in the garden.

3h   Int. Trentwith's sitting room
George, Valentine, Elizabeth

Domestic scene with Elizabeth sewing and George reading the paper, Valentine runs in, then out of the room.

VALENTINE

Here is a letter from uncle Ross to mother.

With a movement of his arm George intercepts the envelope and having opened it starts reading it aloud.

GEORGE

Dear Elizabeth, I spent an enjoyable time with *your son* crab hunting on the beach. It was George's idea, not a bad one. I have received your forgiveness gratefully and accepted your reprimand. Your letter has been prudently destroyed. In faith Ross. *With a broad, satisfied smile he hands the letter to Elizabeth.* My dear, this time **I helped him, thinking of all the times he helped me. Today without me he would have felt lost.** He opened his heart to me: he could not accept what your letter was telling him. I left him with Valentine, a reminder of the consequences of his anger which I try to forgive him for. *(Pause-audible sigh)* Forgiving was not easy for you. This should be the end of the story. We are all keepers of this secret.

ELIZABETH

And the start of a new story: did you not say we are now closer? The keepers of Valentine and of one another, we are shouldering the consequences of our deeds, together, **never alone again.**

GEORGE

Yes: **never again alone.**

The End

THE MERCHANT AND THE GENTLEMAN ON THE EVE OF BRITAIN'S INDUSTRIAL REVOLUTION[62]

The complex psychological battle between Ross and the establishment he is part of but despises, yet will soon rally to, is paralleled by George's relentless scheming (partly socioeconomic partly political) to be part of it. The relationship between component groups of this establishment still unsettled by the memories of civil war is described by Priestland: "Novelists living in the first largely agrarian nation to have experienced the rise of the Merchant have been endlessly fascinated by the tension between the commercial and the agrarian castes… the long running post-Reformation 'culture wars' between the aristocratic 'Cavalier' (who was arrogant, morally lax and cosmopolitan) and the Puritan 'Roundhead' (diligent, moralistic and provincial). Most writers were eager to show how this division could be healed, generally by a wedding" (p.65). This is the case with the marriage between George and Elizabeth. I sense an allegiance of the Author, W. Graham, to the aristocratic culture, despite (or because of) his father being a Mancunian businessman.

Priestland describes a tension between the "hard" merchant (the ruthless, oppressive capitalist) and the "soft" merchant (the paternalistically concerned, caring one). This rests on moral judgements and priorities (after all Adam Smith held a chair of moral philosophy) which come into play here. Ross, the aristocratic warrior, is also the owner of a mine and tries, haphazardly, to develop an industry (smelting copper). He wishes to have control of his mining enterprise but he is threading on the sensitive toes of the Warleggans, a family developing industrial and financial capital ventures. The only wealthy aristocrat not involved in commerce seems to be Lord Falmouth (he has his money "invested in London"), the other aristocrat with money and a pedigree, Francis Basset, is involved in local commercial and financial ventures. Politics attracts all these people for different reasons. Political connections will lead Ross to work in diplomacy and espionage now he is older putting his military experience to good use. Accused in his youth of being a Jacobin and a believer in freedom and democracy he will see the defeat of modest political attempts to improve common people's conditions. His pater-

---

62   Priestland D. 2013.

nalistic aristocratic concerns will lose to the hard merchant's (George) demands for a ruthless, quick capital accumulation in this initial phase of the British industrial revolution; Victorian philanthropy intervened in force only half a century later.

Being a foreigner luckily outside the English class structure and a professional woman who has never taken power and class too seriously (except for learned debates) I do not wish to enter the wider topic of aristocratic values versus the capitalist merchant's work ethic. I am interested in the debate in which George, Ross and Francis Basset intervene (Act 3) in this modified narrative, focusing on the economic tenets opposing hard and soft merchant attitudes; the tension between industry and financial capital is touched on as well. I am concerned by the societal and psychological consequences of backing one or the other viewpoint or possible mixed solutions: the welfare state versus the work house, the iron rice bowl (Chinese communism ensuring a survival diet) versus the "church treasury" (Buddhist and Christian monastic institutions helping the "deserving" poor – and accruing great wealth).

The consequences of surging inequality (in the last 30 years: 1985-2015) on psychological well being, health and social cohesion have been well researched and are shown to be devastating, as indeed they were in late eighteenth century France (but not, apparently, in Britain during the same period). "We have our (bad) ways of dealing with popular discontent" says good old George Warleggan and, historically, he is right. Ross himself must unwillingly collude with rounding up protesters; one of those will be hanged; made an example of. The greater resilience of state structures in Britain in the late eighteenth century may be partly due to a less centralised state organisation (France's aristocracy gained power chiefly by living at Court) served by a local gentry well informed of popular sentiment and keen to maintain their heads attached to their bodies. As noted in W. Graham's Poldark novels the use of state sponsored violence and executions around this time of grave danger for Britain was ruthless (from the hanging judge to the repression of mutinies in the Navy).

There is a discrepancy between religions and morality on this point, religions often ending up theoretically on the side of the oppressed, in practice colluding with/ taking advantage of the oppression. This "religion opium of the people" point is made in the book when timid attempts at protest are quelled by Methodist fervour. Oftentimes religious institutions were the only forces able and willing to protect the oppressed (the biblical term is: "God's poor people"), the grounds for such interventions rooted explicitly in one of the three Abrahamic religions (Judaism, Islam and Christianity) united in their defence of and concern for the poor. Bonhoeffer astutely points out that humanitarian principles cannot stand without their religious foundations, certainly not at times of deep crisis. He is writing during the Second World War in Germany, opposing a triumphant criminal dictatorship. With his customary boldness he states: "It is not Christ who has to justify himself before the world by acknowledging values of justice, truth and freedom. Instead it is these values that find themselves in need of justification and their justification is Jesus Christ…the crucified Christ has become the refuge, justification, protection and claim for these higher values and their defenders, who have been made to suffer". (Ethics, p.345)[63]

It might seem harsh to compare the Nazi regime with the global dominance of hard neo-capitalist values, but the former did at first present an acceptable mask, chocking opposition voices so that an uncovering of its crimes against humanity (deferred by a Nazi policy of killing opponents, covering up the traces of their crimes, burning the evidence and the archives even in their last days) was greeted at first with incredulity. There is ample evidence that multinationals from the twentieth century (IG Farben and Krupp in an alliance with the third Reich) gave support to and colluded with fascist regimes, benefitting in the process; by and large they escaped legal consequences and continued to prosper[64]. The ethical standards of globalised multinationals have been under everybody's eyes long enough and have been commented on after the 2008 crisis making further criticism on my part unnecessary but I cannot resist quoting Plender[65]: "While incomes have stagnated in much of the developed world corporate profit margins are astonishingly high. The role of greed in driving the capitalist money machine seems to have reasserted itself with a vengeance across a corporate sector characterised by a **profoundly disturbing depletion of the stock of moral capital**… This is also a world of great geo-political uncertainty, in which the capitalist mode of production has brought about the industrialisation of warfare and mass killing on a hitherto undreamt-of-scale".

In both Ross and George standards of personal and interpersonal moral codes (or lack thereof) are relevant to their conduct in business and politics. In George's case (as in the *Wall Street* films) freedom from integrity helps him succeed but Ross' good reputation helps his advancement when he becomes able to mediate on his principles. I am unwilling to subscribe to unrealistic ideals, human affairs being ruled by force and reason more than by ethics. I am equally unwilling to believe that the huge benefits of the few and the oppression (close to enslavement) of the majority (even if they can cast a vote every five years) are a sustainable social contract. Present inequality levels are demonstrably damaging[66] to the well-being and happiness of all, even of the lucky few.

Policing the *ethics* of the business world will be done by insiders, the state powers

---

63   Bonhoeffer D. 2005, *Ethics* (1942)

64   Jeffreys D. 2008, *Hell's cartel: IG Farben and the making of Hitler's war machine.*

65   Plender J. 2015, *Capitalism.*

66   Wilkinson R. & Pickett K. 2013, *The Spirit Level.*

and regulators having been, as the technical term states, captured (by those who should be regulated) or, as I say, neutered. Human's most pervasive surveillance is their *conscience*, not always the most effective but oftentimes good enough. I am familiar with the difficulties we all have to acknowledge *reality*, with *modernity*'s discourse around the concept of truth and with the powerful tension towards guilt for sins unknown and for events we did not have the possibility to influence. Dwight comments on his sense of *responsibility* for his inability to save the lives of two children; in such a case the use of the word *guilt* is misplaced yet these feelings are familiar to us all. The "fuzziness" of the *ideas* mentioned above should be borne in mind.

In this script a former ally alarmed by the possibility of becoming George's target, Francis Basset, will start a pre-emptive strike from which George needs to defend himself. George is signalling here that his ethic in the public sphere is changing alongside his private moral code. Ross will only move to help him after he gives a clear indication of such commitment to change. The will and conviction to uphold ethical principles, by agreeing to pay a personal cost apply to both the private and the public life of an individual or they should do. Ricoeur[67] in his tenth Gifford Lecture on the subject of Responsible Self (Le Soi mandate') describes conscience as the possibility to be oneself, to pursue an internal dialogue between the self asking questions and the inner "other" answering them. The inner other is within the self. In his effort to move away from a purely moral view of such internal dialogue and from the image of an inner tribunal judging the self (hopefully leading the will to comply with moral law) he links with Heidegger.

He recalls the expression "the testimony of one's good conscience" (this inner voice becomes a sort of "double") observing that the inner voice attests both the need and the possibility to be true to oneself. As a consequence it is able to judge whether or not the self (having established that it has the capacity and the remit to discriminate good from evil) has indeed followed his own judgement. In everyday experience, the conscience can also affect the self emotionally and punish with the unpleasant feeling of shame but does not have the power to compel the will to conform. This only results from free choice and an exercise of self-control. The opposite outcome is sometimes described as "having lost control of one*self*" when one cannot achieve the behaviour one aims for and does instead what one would like to avoid. George's developing ability to tolerate and make use of an inner dialogue, his need to modify how he is perceived by both himself and others create positive responses around him. He is able to deflect the shaming without defensiveness, with a little self-irony and acceptance of inner as well as social humiliation: "A regrettable state of affairs which I am taking steps to remedy": he is

---

67   Ricoeur P. 2008, *Amour et Justice.*

taking steps to change both the self and his social performance. His surrender is a response to this inner voice's compassionate but severe appraisal which he is able to share with father. Both must overcome shyness and shame: "Who made you aware of your nakedness?" (God's words in Genesis, when Adam and Eve hide and cover themselves in shame after eating the forbidden fruit from the Tree of Knowledge). There is a point in Act 3 d when both George and Ross feel aggrieved, close to a dangerous clash; each understands well the other's state of mind. With a lateral chess move Ross opts for conciliation, refusing to take up George's brazen challenge and using for the first time the word brother. Faced with a defiant George, oscillating between defiance and submission he then reprimands him. George bows to his "brother"[68]. They have now come to feel very close in the class-conscious society of the time despite George's social inferiority complex, a vulnerability which makes accepting the reprimand very difficult for him. This roller coaster has an element of excitement and the thrill of danger.

The intense conflict and the anger in their relationship is not sterilised by the reconciliation, it is verbalised, accepted and mastered. There is a real conflict of interests, divergent aims and strategies: one man represents the former ruling class which is fast losing supremacy and financial standing, the other is a rising power, each bear different values and jousts for social power.

---

68   *Act 3*, end scene d.

Ross Poldark's ethical values, his opinion of Christianity

Ross' return home on the evening of his first political victory (his election as MP for Truro) sees him dissatisfied with himself "Generous and reputable man that I am" he thinks sarcastically. We are at the close of the novel *The Four Swans* by W. Graham.

Some Christian references (which sound to me meaning-less) find their way into an entirely humanistic/stoic/aristocratic code of conduct. The representatives of the church, from Oswald Whitworth to Dr Halse and Reverend Odgers (the local parson) are beneath contempt, uncaring of others when not positively exploitative and downright sadistic, despicably inhuman, often plain stupid. Oswald has entered the Church for want of a better alternative. Halse is described as believing he is practicing mercy and justice when Ross thinks the reverse is true, ironically noting his ability to deliver a stirring sermon on charity at the opening of the new hospital.

A welfare network for the poor based on parishes and infirmaries was in place in the eighteenth century and was being reinforced, the church being involved in education, welfare and the hospitals probably more the province of ruling class philanthropy (Ross enlists Dwight as a doctor for the miners). Demelza's brothers are involved with the Methodist Wesleyan revival seen by the ruling class as dangerously independent from established authority; they are gently teased or caricatured in the Poldark novels as deluded idealists. Politically they had a stabilising influence on the lower classes.

The only person described as convincingly religious is Elizabeth (we see her swearing on the Bible), yet a veil of feigned, empty Christianity covers society's ordering (Ross observes that everybody in Parliament would consider himself a Christian). Sarcastically again he points out how the slave trading activities of the Church of England might be defended by these "good Christians" MPs. The established church and its teachings are seen as part and parcel of the rotten, unethical hypocritical and class bound economic order whose aim is the maintenance of an unjust status quo, even at the risk of triggering an uprising as in contemporary France. Popular unrest is met with a legalised violence of sufficient severity to silence it. Even Ross will have to side with his own class and round up some local people who are identified as cause of the unrest and punish them. His conscience will continue to prick him about this episode; his peers would consider the procedure effective and justifiable.

Ross was thrown back on his own lodestar. It is noted that his father was not a role model and did not intend to be but he loved Ross and his mother whose early loss marks both father and son (his mother taught him some prayers, his only bit of Christianity, lost in the fog of childhood). This infamous father is excluded from polite society as "no woman was safe from his attentions". He dies in poverty, having lost money with mining. Ross' parents have not provided for him financially or emotionally, the moral code offered is evidently flawed. His father has a social ethic: this gives rise in Ross to a yearning for better conditions for the poor and for fairness, not corruption, in politics. He is not however, as he states to Lord Falmouth when the latter offers to sponsor him for the parliamentary seat, a believer in democracy.

The main characters in the story have a traditional sexual ethic (except Valentine who, in the last Poldark novel, is said to resemble Ross' father). Ross initially trying to resist Demelza's naively open seduction even imagines his father calling him "young prude". The double standards of sexual morality for men and women, more prevalent at the time than in modern culture are alluded to but seldom followed. There is a great deal of conversation in the couples about emotions, grievances, tolerance for the other's needs, forgiveness and an effort to understand the partner which echoes the greater openness of the nineteen fifties and sixties both in sexual activity and couple relationships.

The dramatic changes in the balance of power between the sexes and of sexual morality codes started in the First World War picking up speed in the following generation. Medical and psychological ideologies were influencing a field previously dominated by parental guidance, prostitutes, doctors, vicars and their wives. These developments are also visible in the author's skilled handling of the character's detailed exploration of the vagaries of marital happiness, unhappiness and reconciliations. We are told in no uncertain terms that "It is not good for man to be alone, he needs a helpmate" but many snags and snares must be negotiated, shipwreck always a possibility.

The first 7 Poldark novels features (from the point of view of the ethics of relationships and sexuality) humans from the nineteen fifties dressed in eighteenth century costumes. I doubt if any writer can really resurrect the couple relationship patterns of 200 years earlier; were she willing to try the reader might be reluctant to follow her.

Anyone who describes Graham as a proto feminist is, I submit, wrong. There is a line of women targeted by gendered violence of a physical (wife beating, rape, exploitative sex, the murder of a wife due to jealousy) and of a psychological nature (uncaring coldness, adultery, jealous control of the partner) pointing to the contrary. Female characters are keenly observed, with sympathy, but often get the wrong end of the stick. Tension and mounting excitement deriving from the above abuse of women are offered to be enjoyed, with women largely tolerant of it and submissive (or else wanton therefore not respectable even if successfully climbing the social ladder). The author and the reader (man or woman) are thrilled by the chase, the woman (with the possible exceptions of Demelza and Mrs Vosper) being the loser and the victim.

I am reminded of the delicate analysis of romantic and/or sexual relationships in Milan Kundera's novels. I regard the latter author as more carefully observant, more sympathetic to the character's anguish; I fear Graham does not "like" his characters: he exploits then discards them like lovers no longer of interest.

I detect in the humanistic values of fidelity, loyalty, cherishing in good and bad fortune, tolerance and mutual support (as Ross will steel himself to do in the last pages of *The Four Swans*, when Demelza is grieving for the death of his rival for her affections) shadows of the Christian values of charity and forgiveness. An openly religious reading of values in a couple relationship, such as is represented in the attraction between the Methodist preacher (Demelza's brother) Sam and the free spirit, unconventional and unwilling to "convert" Emma is however rejected and the connection is aborted with Emma stating "I am no good for you". I later show how the reason Emma walks away from Sam is, I think, a pointer to the Author's opinion of Christian views of sin and grace.

The contrast between Ross Poldark's value system and George's takes time to emerge and is linked to historical themes: the emerging manufacturing cum financial capital (the Warleggan bank) with its cold, unforgiving, driving efficiency versus the more egalitarian, community oriented, paternalistic values of the landed gentry (who may be involved in mining or politics or fox hunting but whose financial power is declining). The vast, detailed socio-economic historical tableau of this crucial turning point in Britain's socio-economic history[69] seems to me the real purpose and the unique treasure of Graham's novels.

The ethics of relationships to self and others are etched powerfully, if hurriedly and in Ross expose an ethical humanistic warp robbed of a Christian spiritual weft on which the warp was originally threaded[70]. My present attempt to reunite the humanistic warp and the Christian weft, two strands of thought apparently competing for the modern soul, more linked in their roots than their respective advocates may care to observe, will either succeed or, at least partly, fail. What matters to me is that I have tried. The outcome for George in my narrative is set in a Christian frame of reference, the last conversation with his father a version of the prodigal son's Gospel story, his letter relating a spiritual experience of being forgiven by a transcendental figure. Ross' path remains in an agnostic frame, try as I may (try as he may) he does not relate to a transcendent God. Ross remains in an human-

---

69 A turning point for the West and for the history of humanity.

70 I am old enough to have preserved as a childhood memory the image of a huge (to my child's eye) loom where the farmer's wife could weave a bedsheet (hemp was cultivated in the area).

istic ethical frame. His quarrel with God is a moral statement of autonomy and of personal responsibility. He moves in an I-Thou (Martin Buber) logic, making a determined effort to forgive and help George; at times Ross is amazed that he is able to do so. The stumbling block of owning up to his mistakes (integrating them in his self-perception, accepting others' points of view) is overcome with Dwight's and, crucially, with George's help in the end. I have used several quotes from the Bible, a powerful and beautiful text even when taken outside the religious context. My perception is that Ross is not visited by God despite being potentially open for such an encounter[71].

Recent fashions in both psychology and trendy spirituality forming a global web of lukewarm oriental soup with mindfulness and compassion as the main ingredients bear testimony to the desperate need we feel to retrieve some of the religious thread we have lost. I believe the original western item (Christianity) has some time to run before its expiry date and mongrel spiritual fabrications (a travesty of Eastern spiritual heritage) will not even begin to solve this major problem blandly indicated as spiritual needs.

Chapter 10 of *The Four Swans* (the 6th Poldark novel) opens with Ross's reflection on the death of Hugh, a young soldier whom he has saved from a French jail and who has become his rival for Demelza. Both here and later with Elizabeth's death Ross seems unable to tackle the painful shock of mortality early in the course of life. Ross (and the readers) completely forget he has just dealt a crushing blow to George, besting him in the parliamentary election, a fact he will not even mention to his wife. In exasperation he thinks: "So if his affairs had been directed by an old he-goat out of a bog[72] could they have been ordered more perversely? This new adventure he had perversely embarked on…from all sort of ignoble sentiments, not least of them his estrangement from Demelza… Nor had he lost sight of the knowledge that the position he was gaining was the one that George most hated to lose. All exalted motives that would stand him in good stead on the day of Judgement. Generous and reputable man that he was. Why deprive George of his seat if he were full of doubts as to whether he really wanted it? He could not see himself fitting in either with his patron or with the society of England's rulers…"[73]. In this moment of triumph (being elected as an MP) he feels his life and his relationship to Demelza are both in ruins.

A little later, meeting the Methodist minister Sam, he murmurs absentmindedly "If the Lord does not build the house" but immediately dismisses it from his mind.

---

71   The most important people in my adult life and the family I built, my best friends have been (with few exceptions) agnostics; we stopped arguing long ago concerning religion, I continued to observe their spiritual path with interest.

72   "He [the he-goat] looked aggressive, randy, like some old devil come out of the bog".

73   Graham W. 1977, *The Four Swans* (ch. 10).

I doubt many young adults now would recognize this is a biblical line from one of the Psalms (King David's poems, largely, who have inspired countless prayers and music pieces for the last two millennia) which continues: "In vain do the builders labour". In the fifties one could still take such knowledge for granted in an educated middle class. Ross misreads a fundamental biblical concept (one must trust in God's strength, not in one's own) indicating that the God/Devil he-goat is changing his triumph in despair. Sam reveals why he has lost a boxing fight with an opponent (George's hired bully who in the past had badly beaten Drake) "When I was near victory it came to me to think of Christ and how he was tempted by the Devil and of Him being shown all the Kingdoms of the earth… and he refused did not he?" Sam then thinks he should also forego his victory and does so. This same fragment of Christ's temptations is referred to (it was read in church) when Elizabeth agrees to marry George in *Warleggan* ("And the devil said: all the kingdoms of the world and their splendour I shall give to you if you will kneel and worship me. To this Jesus replies: it is written: worship the Lord your God and serve him only")[74]. This quotation can also be seen to underpin George's moral code: a desire for money and power never fully satisfied, leading him to show a brutal disregard for other's emotions, or more precisely to consider others only as instruments to further his own power and success. This is going to be very hard to unpick and remedy in my intended restorative narrative. In W. Graham's novels Ross at times gives a voice to George's absentee conscience.

Let me also note that Sam is giving a personal interpretation of the fragment (both George and his bully may have benefitted from being given a sharp lesson) and let us return to his beloved Emma, the real motive why Sam allows Harry to win the fight. Emma has promised if Sam wins she will start attending his Chapel, they both know her attendance, her belonging to his religious community is necessary for them to come together as a couple. Sam's desire is to leave her an entirely free choice on the matter, but, as Emma confides to Demelza, she hates the feeling of: "Is it being saved – or just be thought a sinner?" The words come from Demelza as Emma seems unable to name these, her feelings.

The triad sin-guilt-grace really sticks in the gullet of the free man and woman living their life to the full within a self-chosen or self-built code of conduct, whose ancestor is Nietzsche's superman. This triad is quite alien to modernity, likewise Bonhoeffer's attempt to root human freedom in Faith with an uncompromising flourish[75] "The daily death of the old self cannot be achieved by anything than

---

74 Gospel of Matthew, Ch.4:8-10. The point of the fragment is: I am the Lord and there is no other, not the rejection of worldly power and riches, unless the latter are automatically identified as coming from the devil.

75 Bonhoeffer D. TF424-25 (DBW 14:11). Quoted in the introduction "Since then everything has changed… it was a great liberation". Submission to the teachings of Jesus became an intense

faith in Jesus". A Lutheran he reverses the direction of travel thus: only Faith>only Grace>go and sin no more[76]. Here may be the core conflict between W. Graham and tenets of Christian ethic. His loyalty is to the aristocratic stance and stoic rectitude maintained by Ross, over and above his several failings which he takes in his stride. In this script the conversation between Dwight and Ross[77] is built around this conflict.

When Ross arrives home he does not find Demelza since she has gone to her friend Caroline to confide her distress about having just heard of Hugh's death. Anger surges in him but when Demelza comes home he subdues his resentment (which is not easy for a man of his temperament) and consoles Demelza, finally holding her, sobbing, in his arms. "'Ross, will you not hold me?' Yes, he said doing it. 'Please hold me and never let me go': 'nor shall I, if you give me the chance'. 'Nor till we die Ross, I could not live without you'". Now, if that is not about Christian forgiveness ("forgiving but not forgetting" understood not as a joke but as a valid standpoint) and mutual understanding and support, such as is found underpinning holy matrimony, what is? Living his marriage brings him very close to living a Christian life, but the experience of Christ as a person he relates to is missing, only partly replaced by his close human encounters. Do we understand the above to be the reaction of a man in love, ready to forgive anything (and Demelza is not asking for forgiveness only, she is asking for his love) or do we see here the strength of a lasting tie and a life shared with a foundation of mutual respect and trust? Are we more aware in a multicultural society of the solid richness of a Christian marriage carried by western culture? This is not to say that a different arrangement, for instance polygamy or civil partnership, would be inferior (as opposed to different). The fact is that monogamous heterosexual western marriage (in its modern incarnation as serial monogamy) has become a point of reference for non-western cultures as well[78]. Close intimate bonds between spouses and long term lovers have been present in all ages and cultures; it was an ancient roman who said that his wife was half of his soul. The point I am trying to make is that even in a determined agnostic like Ross

---

experience of the freedom which he (Bonhoeffer) had longed for.

76   The story of the convicted adulteress, who is to be sentenced to stoning is in John's Gospel chapter 8. The experts of the law are drawing Jesus into choosing between mercy and justice; he turns to them and says: the one amongst you who has no sin may throw the first stone and starts writing in the sand. Like politicians fearing scandalous revelations they all leave one by one and Jesus says to the guilty woman: where are those who condemned you? They are all gone; I shall not condemn you, go and sin no more. It is interesting that she is not told "your sins are forgiven" but she is not condemned.

77   *Act 2*, b.

78   I am aware of making here a controversial claim: I am concerned for the solidity of a core structure of society. I see it not as an isolated nuclear couple but as a wider group spanning three generations and several – linked by blood or by friendship – couples and singles.

(I suppose Graham was too) strands of Christian attitudes and values are needed to guide and make sense of psychological reactions in a context of regret, self-criticism and reconciliation. Ross appears to regret the fact that due to his victory and George's humiliation any chance of mending their feud has disappeared. This is only possible in a culture with a Christian subconscious. He is even concerned that he stood for the parliamentary seat in order to beat George, regarding it as a flawed motivation. His wife says that he seems to be constantly on the dock facing his conscience and mostly returning a guilty verdict on himself. I may be finding Christian roots of this self-deprecating attitude where there are none, but the present solution to his difficulty of owning his victory with a clear conscience can be framed in a Christian attitude of owning riches and power as if one did not own them, because "Where is your treasure there your heart shall be". His treasure and his heart are with Demelza, nothing else matters or is mentioned.

Even George in the early phases of the conflict shows some indication of wanting to remedy the rift, on his terms at least, trying to own Ross just as he has owned Francis with a mortgage on his land and house that Francis will never be able to repay, a house George will later live in with Elizabeth; having been a tolerated guest in his youth there he is now the master. The only reason George will not go for the economic jugular when Francis sides with Ross is that Francis owns someone George desires to possess: Elizabeth. This desire he gives as the reason for his loneliness. I think this isolation has been present since his early years being a painful price he pays for his charmingly polite and ruthless attitude towards others. Finding him emotionally out of reach Elizabeth thinks he has suppressed the expression of his true feelings for so long that he has lost contact with them; he will be lonely in his marriage to her as well. Ross and Demelza, in a stormy intense relationship have long spells of happy companionship and sexual bliss, neither feeling alone for long, a gesture or a word reconnecting to the other.

There may be regret and repentance in the lives of all the people in the story, some forgiveness but little mercy or justice and definitely no conversion or salvation. Unpredictable, arbitrary interventions of the randy He-goat, be it God or devil, help the plot along, like blind fate. I cannot abandon the main characters of this story to this arid gorse filled inner landscape; Dwight did set a fire in an emergency, trying to save Ross from capture: I too, can set fire to the gorse and hope the wind will blow the narrative in the right direction. It is George and with him Ross that I am trying to free, with the consequent releases of Elizabeth and Demelza. Stories can and will be changed by "white swans". I try to follow the characters, the language and culture as they are described in the novels. I maintain the submission of the woman to her husband which now feels dated, showing how, even in this context of an asymmetrical relationship (still prevalent for most of the female population today) there can be mutual openness, listening, comforting and advice running both ways.

ON THE PROCESS OF FORGIVENESS

How glorious it is to be a human being (Kierkegaard, S.)

Much has been written, in the age of Nuremberg trials of Nazis, of military dictators, Truth and reconciliation commissions (in South America and African countries), about sin, guilt and shame, judgement and forgiveness, confession and repentance[79]. The biblical language of forgiveness – kernel of our Christian heritage – has been at times used in a careless and uncritical manner, multiplying rituals on the political stage. I agree with J. Derrida's separation of reconciliation from forgiveness, one not requiring the other; on forgiveness I agree with him on most counts. Psychological understanding of origins and consequences of guilt and shame and of their role in psychotherapy has seen significant progress in the last 50 years. The study of moral development has reappeared in clinical psychology – it was never lost in the study of human development – and I have hopes that the study of will may resurface.

I shall follow the beautiful epilogue *Difficult forgiveness* of Paul Ricoeur's *Memory, History, Forgetting* and the small book by Karl Jaspers (a psychiatrist turned philosopher) *Die Schuldfrage*, on the question of German guilt *(The Guilt Question)* written during the first Nuremberg trial after Second World War.

Ricoeur consistently rejects any claim that the self is immediately transparent to itself or fully master of itself. Self-knowledge only comes through our understanding of our relation to the world and of our life with and among others in our world. We start with the connection between the repentance/confession/judgement and forgiveness processes. A parallel psychological process is building/dismantling/ restructuring the psychological self. The person is both under his/her own gaze and the gaze of the other/s. The self-perception changes, often dramatically. In this story both Ross and George together undergo a parallel process, both are changed by it. This shows an interpersonal, circular process: the fact that George has changed significantly (with the other's help) means that he is also able to help Ross when the latter is locked in his view of events.

My attempt to map the shame to guilt process has partly misfired: a guilt to shame rebound (Ross) was also present. Guilt is deemed a more mature and reparative emotion yet moments of shame were very powerful (when handled compassionately) projecting the subject into altering his behaviour, under the gaze of the shaming

---

79   Lupo J.S. 2010.

other[80]. I was a participant observer of these emotional changes in my characters; I found it riveting and painful during the summer months of 2015. As I said they were going about their business in my head without so much as a "by your leave", a quieter mental clarification started when I felt my characters where at peace; the story complete and plausible. At this experiential level I am tempted to suggest current analytic theories on guilt and shame processes may be too neat and tidy. We should also study the literary masterpieces of modern literature on this topic. Three phases are described:

1. *Confession*: speaking of the wrongs committed, Ricoeur calls it the work *of memory and mourning*. It may be voiced by the perpetrator, or by the victim, by prosecution or witnesses. The task is to outline the facts. It may or may not involve a request for forgiveness. In the third novel (*Jeremy Poldark*) our hero is standing in court accused of leading a riot. The text illustrates beautifully how the legal jargon deadens the charges with monotony and repetition, with hollow solemn words; how both the prosecutor and the accused paint a lively and emotive story with the same facts.

2. *Guilt*: the agent holds himself accountable for the facts committed, this is sometimes a surprise hit for consciousness (Ross). **This experience of fault is in essence a feeling**. The nature of shame is different: it is the experience of the gaze of the other under which one feels exposed. It is a very early, basic and primitively powerful feeling.

3. *Forgiveness* is not predicated on a request by the guilty party, and it bears no relationship to judicial pardon. One may even ask if people are capable of forgiving. **In essence forgiveness is a gift, freely offered**. God's forgiveness is Grace. If man experiences and submits to such Grace (as described in George's letter to Ross) he becomes able to forgive others. Shielded by the other's or God's compassion he becomes able to show compassion to himself. He needs the certainty of forgiveness for repentance and conversion to become possible. Metanoia, the Greek word for conversion translates **beyond mind (not: change of mind)**. Conversion owes more to emotional awareness than to intellectual understanding, at least in the crucial first step.

There are two different ways (not mutually exclusive) of dealing with fault: punishment (the judicial road) and forgiveness, both aim to restore justice, both expect (neither requires, as it cannot force) the guilty party to promise and show the will to reform (self-change). At this point I shall quote H. Arendt: "Men are unable to forgive what they cannot punish and they are unable to punish what has turned out to be unforgivable. This is the true hallmark of those offences which, since

---

80   Shaming can be a tool for oppression and brainwashing: note Bruno Bettelheim's description of its use in Dachau, when he was an inmate there in *The informed heart*.

Kant, we call radical evil" p.241[81]. She is referring to planned mass murder during the Second World War (not a unique event in history, before and since WW2).

The initial meeting, in the cove, is a beginning: a framework is created in which confession and forgiveness take place in safety (There will be no reprisal, no revenge for what is said here today, the other will be treated with respect and kindness but not, automatically, forgiven). Implicit is the notion that the other person is better than his offence. The agent/wrongdoer and his/her action are looked at separately (Ricoeur says it must be possible to separate the agent from his act). The work of memory and mourning unravels a story that is more complicated in George's case as his view of his responsibilities and awareness of his arrogance and selfishness escalate, in parallel with a number of different confessions to different people (even to Valentine). His self-discovery is growing within these dialogues with the other. In his encounter with Drake confession is dispensed with as we see a powerful coming together of a direct request for forgiveness with a direct act of forgiveness (two apparently simple speech acts). The Christian notion of forgiveness stating it is required from the victim who believes he/she has been forgiven by Christ (the fact the enemy does or does not repent being irrelevant) does not automatically lead to the victim feeling that way inclined, as we see with Elizabeth. The idea of forgiveness is at the core of Christianity and has deep roots in the moral foundations of western culture but when it is placed outside its religious frame of reference it can, and often does, appear to be a mindless, sentimental fake.

It is now even questioned whether it is acceptable for the victim (one of Dr. Mengele's twins, survivor from Auschwitz in this instance) Eva Mozes Kor, in her eighties, to forgive an SS corporal Oskar Gröning, in his nineties – repentant. It was her free decision and she observed it led to inner relief from a burden of hate and anger, justified as it was[82]. Public questioning of the faculty to forgive is, today, a very negative message.

Ross is faced with a refusal of forgiveness and seems intent on playing the game on his terms. Both Elizabeth and Dwight will criticize his attempt to evade guilt (accountability of the self for the action committed). He will only be able to overcome his resistance to accepting forgiveness by "letting go" of himself. This is paradoxically linked to his upright character. His inner dialogue with his conscience has been ongoing; his identity is firmly based on building and maintaining his sense of justice and fairness. He has been his own accuser and judge; he prefers to leave it that way. Hearing the prosecution's summing up is a disturbing experience for the person in the dock. Accepting mercy is the same as (or, indeed, even worse

---

81   Arendt H. 1958 *The Human Condition.*The idea of radical evil originally appears in Kant's writings.

82   International Business Times Eva Kor… by Umberto Bacchi on July 15 2015. See also httpd:// en.wikipwdia.org/wiki/Eva_Mozes_Kor

than) accepting blame or sentencing. It all happens outside the tribunal of conscience; the self needs to negotiate a process of acceptance. In Ross, there is a block "I cannot", relieved by the non-judgemental, loving Valentine, by a relaxation of consciousness and of conscience (it is no accident both words share the same linguistic root).

After his fashion, he is a kind and generous man. Many of his dialogues with George prior to the death of Elizabeth contained strong moral undertones. George's response to being reprimanded, despite his self-control, was then predictably catastrophic: he experienced the censure as shaming. Earlier encounters terminate with Ross losing control of himself, which he partly enjoys and partly regrets. Beyond the conflict I sense a curiosity, almost a fascination with each other: a desire to understand someone so very different from oneself.

The distance between acts committed with a clear knowledge of the consequences and acts for which the consequences were unforeseen (when the act was motivated by defensible, if selfish, motives) is debated in the dialogue between George and Elizabeth concerning Morwenna, whose first marriage they arranged. In the end, self-imposed reparation indicates acknowledgement of responsibility by both. Earlier in the story (in the unusual context of Elizabeth not knowing that she has revealed events whilst delirious) a confession on Elizabeth's part is forestalled by George, who declares himself willing to forgive her, taking charge of any talking needed. She will by degrees recover her voice both with him and with Ross, insisting she (the victim) is to be allowed her say. Sexual stereotypes, within cultural norms prevalent at the time are also relevant: her higher social status gives her, in spite of her sex, greater agency.

Ross cannot choose to forgive George: he has to, he is bound by his own need to be pardoned; his generosity towards him indicates he has embraced this necessity. He helps George gain awareness and succeeds because George himself is already well on the road to self-change. Crucially the near death of his wife has lowered the drawbridge to the citadel of his true feelings. George probably felt respect and affection for Ross in the past. Ross suggests he may not have seen positive aspects in George's character, more amenable to change than he anticipated. George concentrates on grappling successfully with some attitudes of his he condemns during the conversation with his father: his need to dominate and his manipulative lying. His father replies his faults are also, partly, his strength. Ross finds understanding and unconditional support in Demelza, herself struggling with her sense of inferiority with regards to Elisabeth and with the personal wound of knowing Ross has given Elizabeth a child (the blue-eyed Valentine). This is a shame Ross is vulnerable to (at several points George will use this weapon). George has no choice (in this historical context) but to try and forgive = forget the fact and accept Valentine as his wife's child, keeping up the deceit. He needs a legitimate heir. He regards this both as a challenge and as a penance. At several points in the narrative he is forcing himself to bend to the other (Ross chiefly). This is a complete change of direction for a person who used to concentrate his skills on making others bend to him. Ross' change of direction contains more irritation, less willpower and more letting go. It involves I think letting go of the remorse which is morally paralysing him, making an acceptance of his being at fault in *details* nearly unbearable. His wife offers him sympathy and support, conditional to shielding or repairing their relationship. This is also evident in the original novels where two major reconciliations of Ross and Demelza are sensitively described.

It has been said the devil is in the details, it certainly is in the process of confession/forgiveness. Nether may not be forced, nor enforced. A so called Christian standard response to murder and terrorism (we all forgive everything at once) shows devastating, hypocritical stupidity which damages the possibility of sincere forgiveness. This possibility, indeed this desire, is always present in humans and is mentioned in ancient, more unforgiving times as a princely prerogative: mercy. The verdict clearing Ross of the sedition charge (potentially fatal, as George, who has instigated and supported the legal process, knows) according to the words of the peeved judge owes more to the mercy than to the logic of the jury. Ross will later describe himself as law abiding. This is partly ironic but partly true. His marital happiness with Demelza and the mercy of the jury (during the trial he has to be restrained by Counsel from near suicidal angry sincerity) have led to his acceptance of the need for restraints and judicial control over a society which he continues to condemn as cruel and corrupt. He will try and fail to obtain changes in the direction of greater social justice in his role as an MP. The Napoleonic wars trumped all other agenda items. When it was over Britain found itself the global dominant power: what need or incentive was there then to yield power or control on the part of the ruling classes?

One can see the process of awareness (confession) unrolling with George as Ross tries to maintain in their relationship an active process of forgiveness, responsive to George's need for help (when he hints at suicidal despair) and even to his implied request for friendship. Ross has to master desires to take advantage of his being dominant in this new, alarmingly intense and unstable relationship. Neither is above taunting the other when the occasion presents itself but the frame of respect and reconciliation established during the dialogue on the beach is adhered to. There are moments of judgement, spoken to the self or spoken to the other. Words here assume the weight of a speech act; words become incisive and memorable, requiring response. I hear the objection that people do not speak as they do in this play but I maintain that they can and will.

The process leads to a better psychological awareness of self and other but gives little attention to normative and legal (societal) facets. Ross, for example, has committed indictable actions (the duel, the rape); from a legal point of view he gets away, in himself he does not. Formal justice by itself can become sterile and impotent. The relationship of justice to forgiveness is vitally important: within her/his acceptance of guilt both (justice and forgiveness) are desired by the wrongdoer as much as by everyone else. Upholding justice is necessary for the survival of a human community but mercy is equally crucial, opening up a space for a justice freed from legality. Many actors in this dialogue start from or arrive at forgiveness, born from awareness of one's own poverty: this is clear in Elisabeth's change of heart.

Forgiveness has become the subject of philosophers' debate in French culture starting with Ricoeur, Jankelevitch (the former a Christian, the latter a Jew) and Derrida. My present sense of urgency (see the introduction) is explained by the following quote on modernity which comes (I think) from Jean Baudrillard and gives the breadth of a wider theme this play is alluding to, the work of memory and mourning becoming an historical task, digging the garden for the corpses and seeking a criminal uncomfortably close to home:

"History backtracks on its own footsteps in a compulsive attempt at rehabilitation, as if in a recompense for some sort of crime I am not aware of – **a crime committed by and in spite of us, a kind of crime done to oneself, the process of which is sped up in our contemporary phase of history and the sure signs of which today are global waste, universal repentance and resentment** – a crime where the lawsuit needs to be re-examined and where we have to be unrelenting to go back as far as the origins, if necessary, in quest of retrospective absolution since there is no resolution to our fate in the future. It is imperative that we find out what went wrong and at which moment and then begin examining the traces left on the trail leading up to the present time, to turn over all the rocks of history, to revive the best and the worst in a vain attempt to separate the good from the bad. **Following Elias Canetti's hypothesis we have to return to this side of the fatal line of demarcation which, in history, has kept the human separate from the inhuman, a line that we, at some point, have thoughtlessly crossed under the spell and vertigo of some sort of anticipated liberatory effect**".

Bianca Rosa Hart
Redhill, Surrey, August 15th 2015

What's in a Pen Name?

A **nom de plume** is an old fashioned, pathetic artifice in these internet days when everything is revealed, as in the Day of Judgement but I have condensed so much in this pen name that I cannot let it go.

Bianca is the main character in George Bernanos's screenplay *The Last One to the Scaffold*, the libretto of Poulenc's Opera *Dialogues des Carmelites*. A Carmelite nun of noble birth Bianca dies guillotined in the course of the French revolution, during which she had been hiding, petrified with fear. In the end, she will find her courage.

Rosa is Rosa Luxemburg, the Marxist economist murdered with her partner by right wing militias in 1919 Germany during the (Marxist) Spartacist uprising; she said the revolt was a mistake and she was right!

Die Weisse Rose (translates in Italian Rosa Bianca) was the name of a secret student group in Ulm which started some opposition to the regime during the Second World War. Arrested by the German police the brother and sister Hans and Sophie Scholl were then guillotined.

Works Cited

Al-Ghazali, A.H. (2005) *La Bilancia dell'Azione.* Torino, UTET.

Arendt, H. (1958) *The Human Condition.* Chicago University Press.

Bernanos, G. (1949) *The Carmelites' dialogue.*

Bonhoeffer, D. (1996) *Discipleship.* (Nachfolge, 1937) Minneapolis, Fortress Press.

Bonhoeffer, D. [2005 (1942)] *Ethics.* Minneapolis Fortress Press.

Bonhoeffer, D. (1988) (*Letters from Prison.* Munchen, Kaiser Verlag) *Resistenza e Resa.* Milano Edizioni San Paolo.

Broughton, G. (2015) *Restorative Christ. Jesus, Justice and Discip leship.* Cambridge,The Lutterworth Press.

Jeffries, D. (2008) *Hell's Cartel: IG Farben and the making of Hitler's warmachine.* Metropolitan books.

Fest, J. (2007) *Albert Speer, conversations with Hitler's Architect.* USA, Polity Press.

Graham, W. (1977) *The angry Tide,* a novel of Cornwall. London Macmillan.

Graham, W. (1977) *The Four Swans.* London Macmillan.

Plender, J. (2015) *Capitalism.* London Biteback Publishing Ltd.

Jaspers, P. (1965 (1946)) *Die Schuldfrage.* Munchen, R.Piper&co.

Lupo, J.S. (2010) *Can we be forgiven? On "impossible" and "communal" Forgiveness in Contemporary Philosophy and Theology.* http://scholarworks.gsu.edu/rs_theses, Georgia State University,2010.

Ricoeur, P. (2000) *The Just.* Chicago, University of Chicago Press.

Ricoeur, P. (2004) *Memory, History, Forgetting.* Chicago, University of Chicago Press.

Ricoeur, P. (2004) *Evil, a challenge to Philosophy and Theology.* London, Continuum.

Ricoeur, P.[2004(1985)] *Le Mal.* Genève, Labor et Fides.

Ricoeur, P. (2008) *Amour et Justice.* Paris, Editions Points.

Priestland, D. (2013) M*erchant, Soldier, Sage. A new History of Power,* London, PenguinBooks.

Rawls (1971) *A Theory of Justice.* Oxford Paperbacks.

Tusa, A.T. (1984) *The Nuremberg Trials.* London, Macmillan.